PRAISE FOR THE NOVELS OF
OPAL CAREW

"With deft attention to detail . . . and a flirtation with the forbidden . . . this pleasing love story will satisfy romance fans." —*Publishers Weekly*

"A must-read . . . Carew definitely knows how to turn up the heat." —*RT Book Reviews*

"Carew brings erotic romance to a whole new level. . . . She sets your senses on fire!"

—*Reader to Reader*

"You might find yourself needing to turn on the air conditioner because this book is HOT! Ms. Carew just keeps getting better." —*Romance Junkies*

"A dip in an icy pool in the winter is what I needed just to cool off a little once I finished this yummy tale!"

—*Night Owl Reviews* (5 stars)

"Whew! A curl-your-toes, hot and sweaty erotic romance. I didn't put this book down until I read it from cover to cover. . . . I highly recommend this one."

—*Fresh Fiction*

"Carew is truly a goddess of sensuality in her writing."
—*Dark Angel Reviews*

"Carew pulls off another scorcher. . . . She knows how to write a love scene that takes her reader to dizzying heights of pleasure." —*My Romance Story*

W9-CEI-800

ALSO BY OPAL CAREW

A Fare to Remember
Big Package (e-novella)
Nailed
Meat (e-novella)
My Best Friend's Stepfather
Stepbrother, Mine
Hard Ride
Riding Steele
His to Claim
His to Possess
His to Command
Illicit
Insatiable
Secret Weapon
Total Abandon
Pleasure Bound
Twin Fantasies
Swing
Blush
Six
Secret Ties
Forbidden Heat
Bliss

Heat

Opal Carew

WITHDRAWN

St. Martin's Griffin

New York

Orange County Library System
146A Madison Rd.
Orange, VA 22960
(540) 672-3811 www.ocplva.org

This is a work of fiction. All of the characters, organizations, and events portrayed in this novel are either products of the author's imagination or are used fictitiously.

HEAT. Copyright © 2017 by Opal Carew. All rights reserved. Printed in the United States of America. For information, address St. Martin's Press, 175 Fifth Avenue, New York, N.Y. 10010.

www.stmartins.com

The Library of Congress Cataloging-in-Publication Data is available upon request.

ISBN 978-1-250-11678-9 (trade paperback)
ISBN 978-1-250-11679-6 (e-book)

Our books may be purchased in bulk for promotional, educational, or business use. Please contact your local bookseller or the Macmillan Corporate and Premium Sales Department at 1-800-221-7945, extension 5442, or by e-mail at MacmillanSpecialMarkets@macmillan.com.

First Edition: June 2017

10 9 8 7 6 5 4 3 2 1

To Rose,
Thank you for everything!
I wish you great success and joy!

Acknowledgments

Thank you to Rose Hilliard, who was my wonderful editor for eleven years. (I'll miss you!) And thanks to Emily Sylvan Kim, my fabulous agent, who's always in my corner. And as always, thank you to Mark, Matt, and Jason for their loving support.

Heat

Chapter One

"Firemen? *Naked?*"

Rikki stared at her friend Cassie, her jaw open.

"Why not? You want to get more work as a photographer. And this'll be way more fun than just snapping pictures of schoolkids and doing grad photos."

"But shots for a calendar of naked firefighters?" Rikki's cheeks blazed with heat. She had never even seen a naked man, let alone casually taken a picture of one.

"Okay, they won't be *totally* naked. Just bare chests." Cassie grinned. "Enough to show off their big muscles."

"I don't know. They'll be taking off their clothes. I'll be alone with them taking pictures. They might think that . . ." Rikki bit her lip. "I mean . . . maybe they'll get ideas."

"Not with the big 'don't touch' sign you have hanging over your head. Honey, I've seen how you freeze out men."

"I don't mean to," Rikki practically stuttered. But she knew what Cassie meant.

Cassie leaned in close. "So think about it this time and

don't put up those shields. Believe me, these are all really nice guys. Why not actually let yourself get involved with one of them?"

Rikki's stomach clenched. "Oh, Cassie. You know I can't do that. Not with a fireman."

"You *could*." Cassie squeezed her hand. "I know with what happened to you . . . the way you lost Jesse . . ." She pursed her lips, compassion in her eyes. "But you haven't been in a serious relationship ever since . . . unless you've been holding out on me."

Rikki shook her head. It was true.

"So you need to move forward. And it will probably be really good for you to do it with a fireman. Just to get over that block you have. So why not let yourself be okay with having a fling with one of these guys? That would probably be the best thing for you. Just a meaningless sexual relationship to help you get your groove back."

Rikki shook her head. "I don't think so."

"Okay." Cassie patted Rikki's hand. "Maybe not with a fireman then. But I could introduce you to some other nice guys in town. Just think casual relationship and see where it goes from there. Maybe a nice guy to show you around."

Rikki had only just moved to town. She and Cassie had been friends since college, but this was the first time since then that they'd lived in the same city.

"I'm actually going out with my roommates on Thursday evening."

"Oh, that's great. How's it going with that?"

Rikki didn't know her roommates. She needed to keep

costs down, so she'd answered an ad for a room in a town-house with three other people.

"I've only met Tina so far." Rikki had moved in yesterday and Tina, who had the bedroom next to hers, was the one who'd let her in. "She's really friendly and seems like she'll be fun. She suggested we all go out for drinks together so I can get to know them."

"Where are you going?" Cassie asked.

"Somewhere called Rango's."

Cassie's eyebrow darted up. "That's kind of a pickup place."

"Oh. Well, maybe Tina doesn't know that. Or maybe I got the name wrong."

Cassie laughed. "Or maybe she sized you up right away and figures you need to get laid. Anyway," she continued before Rikki could protest, "about this calendar, I really hope you'll do it."

Rikki hesitated. She hated to say no to Cassie.

Cassie leaned closer. "How can you turn down an opportunity like this? It'll allow you to do something you love—taking fabulous photographs—and it'll help raise money for the firemen's fund. A very worthwhile cause. They do all kinds of great things for the neighborhood."

Rikki pursed her lips. Why did Cassie have to be so persuasive?

Cassie laughed. "You know you want to. Just say yes."

"I suppose I could meet with them and see what they're looking for."

"Actually, I'm the one managing the whole thing for them. My dad and the chief are old friends and ever since I was a kid, our whole family used to help out at the fund-raisers. So now I'm volunteering my publicist talent to them."

"Oh, no. That means I'm volunteering, too, right?"

"Well, you're between jobs right now, so you have the time. And I had a great idea. You know I have a few author clients who would be thrilled to have original photos of sexy guys for their book covers rather than the same-old-same-old stock art. Sooo . . . I suggested to the guys that in exchange for your time, they agree to let you take extra shots of them, and they'll give you the rights to use their images. That means you can start building up a portfolio of pictures of sexy, half-naked men."

At Rikki's dubious expression, Cassie added, "You can probably charge anywhere from four to six hundred dollars per image as long as you make them exclusive to the author."

"You think your author clients will actually spend that much?"

"I believe they will. And one of them is just starting a new series, so that could turn into five or more covers right off the bat. She totally trusts my judgment, and I have total confidence in your ability."

"Okay, I guess I can't really say no."

Rikki's fingers curled around the sheets as she lay in her dark bedroom, images of a big, muscular man carrying an axe, his naked chest dripping with perspiration, gliding through her brain. The ridges of his muscles gleamed in the light of the fire. His face was smudged with soot and the curved lines of his fireman's hat complemented the masculinity of his angular face.

Damn, ever since Cassie had suggested Rikki do this calendar project, Rikki had been swamped with sexy dreams of firemen. Stripping naked in front of her. Their cocks hanging free. And their cocks were always *sooo big*. Big enough to be downright daunting.

She shook her head. Of course they'd be daunting. Any size would be daunting to her, given her limited experience.

Extremely limited experience. She closed her eyes again, but all she could think about were big, sexy firefighters. Ripped and full of testosterone. Sleeping in a firehouse together. Showering together. Their big naked bodies glistening with water.

Oh, God, she could feel her body reacting. The melting heat between her legs. The aching need inside her.

She glided her fingers over her breast, then down between her legs. The flesh there was slick and needy and her stomach tightened. She stroked a couple of times, then allowed her fingertip to graze the little bud buried in the folds, and wild sensations burst through her.

No!

She pulled her hand away and rolled onto her stomach, burying her face in the pillow. She wasn't going to do this again. It was pointless and frustrating. She suspected there was something physically wrong with her. It took forever to give herself an orgasm, and even then, she wasn't entirely sure that was what she was experiencing.

She dug her fingers into the pillow, frustration flooding through her veins. Why did she have to be so totally incompetent in her sexuality?

"Hey, roomie." Tina looked up from her bowl of cereal. "There's coffee in the pot."

"Thanks." Rikki shuffled to the pot, tired from her restless night, and poured herself a cup, then sat across from Tina.

Tina had bright blue eyes, always full of curiosity—and a dash of mischief—and short honey-blonde curls with a shock of hot pink, violet, and vivid peacock blue. Her nails were impeccably done to look like shiny black talons, coming to a sharp point at the end, with an intricate silver design etched on top. She even had a tiny silver skull charm, dangling from a ring pierced through one nail tip, the whole thing about a quarter inch long.

Tina worked at a trendy boutique along the lakeshore where a lot of tourists shopped. Muldone was a tourist town along a beautiful lake with a lovely view of the mountains.

One of their other roommates, Anna, worked in the same area, but in a store with fancy soaps. Some were beautiful, but not too practical, like the ones shaped like cupcakes, teacups, even wedding cakes—all life-size. The ones Rikki liked were the round ones marbled in different colors with a soft scent.

"Are you off to work soon?" Rikki asked.

Tina wore a tiny black leather skirt and a form-fitting shirt that accentuated her slim waist and dipped low enough in front to give an eyeful of cleavage. The necklace she wore nestled between her breasts, the sparkle of the stone drawing attention right to them. Rikki was sure a man wouldn't be able to take his eyes off the soft rounded curves. Rikki found it difficult herself.

"Can't help looking at the girls, eh?" Tina leaned forward, exposing even more breast. "I don't mind, but just to warn you, I'm not into women myself."

Rikki's eyes widened. "Oh, no . . . I didn't mean . . ." She tugged her gaze from Tina's breasts, feeling her cheeks heat.

Tina laughed. "Don't worry about it. I'm teasing. But I don't care who or what you're into. Whatever it is, though, I think you need to get yourself some soon. I heard you moaning in your sleep. I mean," she quirked her head, "unless you're hiding a guy in your room. If so, dump him, because he didn't seem to be taking you where you needed to go."

Oh, God! Tina had heard her during her steamy dreams? Her cheeks heated even more.

"Been a while, has it?" Tina asked.

Rikki sipped her coffee, more to block her face with the cup. "I really don't want to talk about this."

"Yeah, okay." Tina stood up. "But don't worry. I've got your back." She put her dishes in the dishwasher, then walked to the door. "See you at Rango's at eight."

Simon leaned back against the bar and checked out the crowd. His best friend Carter sat on the tall stool beside his. They didn't usually come to places like this, but both of them had been suffering from a dry spell lately and this was the best place in town to find a sexy, willing woman.

They both wore casual clothes—short-sleeved cotton shirts and presentable jeans—unlike most of the guys in the place who wore shirts and ties and even full suits. When hanging out during their time off, they liked to be comfortable, and any woman who didn't like that wasn't right for them.

His gaze flicked to the young woman walking into the bar. She gazed around hesitantly and nothing about her seemed to fit this scene. Instead of a fashionable short dress with plunging neckline and stiletto heels, she wore a floral sundress with soft, flowing lines that floated around her legs as she walked. He could just imagine a soft breeze lifting the hem and showing more of her long, shapely legs.

The sandals she wore were feminine and sexy, made up of thin leather straps hugging her pretty feet. The heels were high, but not six-inch spikes like what so many of the other women wore. And her toenails were painted a deep peachy-pink tone. The sunny color made him smile.

As his gaze glided back up her body, he couldn't help noticing the flare of her hips accentuating her narrow waist, and the scooped neckline of her dress giving the merest glimpse of the soft breasts beneath. Her hair—a long, straight curtain of glossy deep-auburn—cascaded past her shoulders halfway to her waist.

He loved long hair on a woman. Loved to coil his hand in it and tug her head back so he could nuzzle her throat. Maybe get a little rough if she was into that.

But this woman . . . He couldn't see himself doing that to her. She seemed too vulnerable somehow. He could see running his fingers through those silky strands. Gliding them behind her ear, then drawing her face close and kissing those full, pouty lips.

Her face—so sweet and angelic—was heart-shaped with a pert little nose and eyes so big he could get lost in them.

"Goddamn!" Carter nudged him and Simon realized his friend was looking at the same woman. "Man, I know you saw her a split-second before I did, but maybe with this one we could go for a team effort."

Simon turned to Carter. "She doesn't look like the type who would be into that. In fact, I'm surprised she's in a place like this in the first place."

"But she is." Carter grinned. "And it's the quiet ones that'll surprise you most."

Simon turned back to look at her again. She'd sat down at a table with three other people: two women and a man.

"Maybe. Or maybe she's here with that guy."

Carter took a sip from his beer stein. "We'll see."

Rikki felt a little out of place. Tina was wearing the same short skirt and low-cut top she'd worn to work today and Anna was dressed similarly in a short royal blue dress that barely kept her breasts contained. Mel, their male roommate, wore black dress pants and a dark shirt. Very sleek looking.

Anna was a petite brunette, a little shorter than Tina. She was quieter than Tina and stayed in her room a lot but was friendly enough. Mel was a good-looking guy. Tall with short, sandy blond hair and a crooked smile. She'd only seen him a couple times at the house since she'd moved in. He worked odd hours and seemed to go out with his friends a lot.

"Hi, Rikki," Anna said. "I brought you this." She handed Rikki a gift bag with neon stripes and lime green tissue paper. "It's a welcome gift."

Rikki reached into the bag and pulled out something wrapped in the lime tissue and set it on the table, then carefully unwrapped it. It looked like a tall, fluffy slice of strawberry shortcake.

"It's soap," Anna said. "Smell it."

Rikki lifted it and breathed in the delicate aroma of strawberries and vanilla.

"Thanks, Anna. That's very nice."

"Here, I got you something, too." Tina handed her a small package that fit in her palm. It was wrapped in black tissue with a red heart-shaped holographic sticker holding the edges together.

Rikki opened it to find a silver mesh coin purse inside. "That's really cute. Thank you."

"Wait," Tina said with a grin. "Look inside."

Rikki flicked open the top and peered inside. She pulled out something black. Lace. She started to hold it up, but then clamped her hand around it when she realized it was a thong.

Tina tugged it from her hand and laid it on the table. There was barely anything to it. Just a triangle of lace at the front and a smaller one at the back with thin strings attaching them. Tina slid her hand under the larger triangle then pushed her finger through the middle and wiggled it.

"They're crotchless."

Rikki's gaze darted around them, wondering if the other patrons were staring at this wicked gift, but luckily the gift bag from Anna's present blocked it from most people, and the few people around them who would have a clear view weren't paying any attention.

Mel laughed. "They're crotch*less* and back*less*. There couldn't be much *less* of them." He grinned. "I like."

Rikki crumpled them in her hand and stuffed them back in the coin purse, then slipped it into her bag.

"Uh . . . thank you?"

Tina laughed and winked at Anna. "I told you I could make her cheeks turn bright red."

"Yeah, okay, so here's your ten bucks," Anna said, pulling a bill from her purse and handing it to Tina.

"Are you guys always like this?" Rikki asked.

Tina shrugged. "We like to have fun with each other."

"Yeah, it would have been fun if you'd let me know you were bringing gifts," Mel said.

"That's easily fixed," Anna said. "Why don't you just buy a round of shots, then order Rikki a special drink after that?"

"Great idea." Mel signaled to a waitress and ordered. A few minutes later, the waitress returned with four full shot glasses and set them on the table. Tina and Mel tipped theirs back.

Anna picked up hers and glanced at Rikki. "Ready?"

Rikki lifted hers, too, and nodded, then tipped it back at the same time as Anna.

She swallowed the whole thing, just as the others had. She tried not to react to the burn down her throat, but she wasn't used to this kind of thing so she winced a little.

Tina nudged her arm with a smile. "Want another?"

"Maybe later," Rikki said.

Simon signaled to the bartender and she came over.

"Rhonda, we'd like to send a drink over to that woman in the sundress. The one with the gift bag on the table. Do you know what they're celebrating?"

"Yeah, I know her friend Tina. It's some kind of welcome gift. I think she just moved to town."

"Great. And you probably know what kind of drink she'd like, too, right?"

"You know it." She leaned forward, giving an eyeful of her curvy breasts in her low-cut tank top. "And before you ask, the guy isn't her boyfriend, so no competition there. Not that any guy here could compete with either of you." She grinned and winked.

"Yeah, I bet you say that to all the guys," Carter said.

"Sure." Her eyes twinkled. "But with you two, it's true."

Simon laughed as Rhonda walked away, a seductive sway to her hips.

"So she's new in town, which probably means no guy in the picture," Carter said. "We've got a shot."

"Yeah, but you or me?"

Carter grinned. "I could just wander over there and ask her."

Chapter Two

"Hot guy heading this way," Anna said.

Rikki's gaze shot to the tall, dark-haired man in the snazzy blue suit walking toward their table, his gaze locked on her. Anxiety rippled through her and she dropped her gaze to her empty glass, then glanced to the side. When he arrived at the table, instead of talking to Rikki as she'd feared he would do, he asked Anna to dance.

Once they were gone, Tina turned to her. "How did you do that?" She leaned in closer. "And more importantly, *why* did you do that?"

"Do what?" Rikki asked.

"That guy was absolutely going for you," Tina said.

"That's the truth," Mel chimed in.

"But at the last minute, after you put up that cold front, he changed his mind."

"I didn't—"

"Yeah, you did," Mel said. "Any guy would turn away frostbitten from that glacial look."

"Didn't you find him attractive?" Tina asked.

Rikki glanced at the man as he danced with Anna. "Yeah, I guess so, but I don't want to be picked up in a bar."

"Really? I think one-night stands can be liberating. No strings. No expectations. Just fun sex." Tina nudged her arm. "Maybe it'll do you good."

"Heads-up, ladies," Mel said. "Here comes another one."

Tina and Rikki both glanced at another suited man heading toward them.

"Oh, he's cute. I saw him earlier and was hoping to catch his attention." Tina leaned in close to Rikki. "You know, if you want to do that ice queen thing one more time, I won't mind."

The man was clearly glancing at Rikki. Self-consciously, she glanced down at her drink again. She didn't know exactly what she did to scare off men, but she hoped this guy would talk to Tina instead of her.

Seconds later, Tina was following him onto the dance floor.

"Mission accomplished," Mel said with a smile.

Rikki noticed that Mel kept glancing to the bar and she realized that a woman was giving him the eye.

"Hey, Mel, you don't have to stay here with me if you want to go and talk to that woman."

He glanced at the woman and she sent him a seductive smile. He was obviously interested, but he sat back in his chair and smiled at Rikki.

"No, I don't want to abandon you. I wouldn't want you to feel uncomfortable sitting here all by yourself."

"That's okay. Anna and Tina will be back soon anyway."

"Actually, Anna went to sit with her guy at his table. She just texted to let me know."

Damn.

"Really, it's okay. I'll be fine," she insisted. She did not need a babysitter.

"All righty then. But just so you're ready for it, I think one of those two guys at the bar will be over here next."

She couldn't help it. Her gaze flicked to the bar and landed on a tall, broad-shouldered man with a beer in his hand. At the first sight of his broad shoulders and thick, muscular biceps, her breath caught. He was just so masculine and virile looking. His eyes glowed with interest as she gazed his way. Electricity crackled through her, curling her toes and sending her heart into palpitations.

She tried to drag her gaze away, but she couldn't. He smiled and her heart stuttered.

Shock jolted through her at the intensity of the feelings flooding through her. That this was the man she was meant to be with.

It was a feeling she'd had only once before.

When she'd met Jesse.

She dragged her gaze back to her drink and took a sip, her hand shaky.

"You okay?" Mel asked, his gray eyes lit with concern. "You know that guy?"

"No, I've never seen him before."

"But . . . ?" Mel prompted.

"But . . . sometimes I get feelings about people and . . ." She shrugged.

His lips turned up. "And this guy gives you very *special* feelings, I take it."

She wasn't about to explain that this was more than just an illicit attraction. Most people didn't get it.

Her mother had always told her that many of the women in their family had a strong intuition about certain things. In fact, that they were a bit psychic. She'd explained that it was stronger in some than others and Rikki had assumed she didn't have it at all, because she'd never had any real premonitions, or anything like that. And then she'd met Jesse and that strong sense of *rightness* had blazed through her.

Just like it did now.

But she couldn't believe she was having this kind of feeling for some guy in a bar.

"You should just go do your thing," Rikki said.

He laughed, then stood up. "Whatever you say."

As soon as Mel left, the waitress showed up with a drink. It was tall and slushy with a spear of fruit on top.

"From the two gentlemen at the bar. They said to say welcome to Muldone."

Rikki's gaze shot to the bar, and the man she'd been gazing at before smiled and nodded. Then she glanced at the man next to him and—

It was like a punch to the gut. That same intense feeling as she'd had when she'd seen the first man. That *this* was the man she was meant to be with.

This guy had the same type of physique as the first. Tall,

muscular. Very strong. His hair was a soft brown, and wavy. She imagined it would feel soft to the touch. And his eyes seemed very warm.

His gaze shifted from his friend to her for the first time and—Wham! Instant electricity.

Oh, God, how could she have the same feeling—this very special and intense intuitive feeling—for two men?

Of course, she couldn't. She was just reading things wrong.

The two men stood up and started to walk her way. Her heart fluttered, then started pounding faster as they approached the table.

"Hello. My name is Simon," the first man said. "And this is my friend, Carter."

"Hi," Carter said.

Simon held out his hand and she shook it. At the first touch, sparks flared through her body, playing havoc with her senses. Then she shook Carter's hand, and had the same wild reaction.

"Hi, uh . . . I'm Rikki."

"May we join you?" Carter asked.

Ordinarily, she would make some excuse to send them away, but she was too befuddled and found herself nodding.

"I . . . uh . . . thanks for the drink."

Simon smiled. "Our pleasure."

"How did you know I just moved to town?"

Carter laughed. "Rhonda on the bar knows her clientele. She told us."

Rikki nodded and took a sip of the icy drink, and the sweet flavor of peaches exploded on her tongue.

"It's delicious."

"So did your party break up," Simon asked, "or will the others be coming back?"

"I'm not really sure. I'm not used to coming to places like this, but I think they might have moved on." She could see Tina sitting at another table, and Mel leaning in close to the woman he was talking to at the bar.

"So the guy just ditched you?" Simon asked.

She shrugged. "He's not my boyfriend or anything. In fact, I barely know him. We just live together."

At Simon's arched eyebrow, she added, "He's my new roommate. All three of them are. But I just met them when I moved in a few days ago."

"Well, since they've moved on, do you want to go somewhere quieter where we can talk?" Carter asked.

Anxiety quivered through her. These guys were definitely moving faster than she liked.

"Don't look so panicky," Carter said. "I just mean we could move to a booth on the back wall. With the overhang, it's quieter and we won't have to fight with the music to hear each other."

"Oh." She glanced to the wall and saw a few booths were open. "That would be okay."

She stood up and grabbed her purse and her gift from Anna. Simon picked up her drink and he and Carter followed her to one of the booths. As soon as she sat down, she noticed the difference in noise level.

"You're right, this is better," she said.

The two men sat across from her in the rectangular booth.

"I'll just let my friends know where I am." She grabbed her phone and texted Tina.

Way to go, Tina texted back with a winky face.

"So where did you move here from?" Carter asked.

"I was in Ashton. That's the small town in Ohio where I grew up. But I got laid off from work and so I decided to start again someplace new."

"And you came here because of the great scenery?" Simon asked.

"It is a beautiful spot. I hadn't realized how pretty it was here or how much of a tourist destination it is. I came here because a close friend from college lives here and I thought it would be fun if we lived in the same place again."

"Friends are important." Carter's smile caused his eyes to twinkle.

"You two are good friends, I take it," she observed.

"That's the truth," Simon said.

"Yeah. We share everything."

The glitter in Carter's eyes sent a shiver of excitement through her. As if he'd just told her that he and Simon both wanted to be with her. To kiss her . . . undress her . . . make love to her. Together.

Oh, God, the thought of being with one of these big, muscular men was enough to steal her breath away. But the thought of being with *both* of them . . .

Of course, she was just being silly. Because of the weirdness of her intuitive feeling that she was meant to be with Simon. And with Carter. She was misinterpreting things. They probably shared an apartment and maybe a car and . . . whatever else guys shared on a regular basis.

Not women.

Not her.

"Do you have a job lined up?" Simon asked.

"Oh, no. I have a little savings and I moved in with three roommates to save money while I get things going. My college friend has a small business and I'll do some work for her. If that doesn't bring in enough, then I might take a retail job for a while."

She didn't really want to talk about work. She sounded like a dreamer who couldn't hold down a job. Or a loser, her brother would say. She hadn't even told him she'd moved to Virginia. He lived in California anyway and barely ever called. Mom and Dad would tell him.

"Where are you both from?" she asked.

"I lived in an even smaller place than this, about an hour north of here. I moved to Muldone about six years ago," Simon said.

"And I've lived here all my life. It was a great place to grow up. With being right on the lake I practically lived at the beach in the summer. And in the winter, I'd head up to the mountains to snowboard. We even took school trips for downhill skiing sometimes. I love it here."

Carter was so animated when he talked about Muldone, his eyes twinkled. She could watch him all day.

The waitress arrived and set down a small, stemmed liqueur glass in front of Rikki.

"This is from a guy named Mel," the waitress said as she placed their empty glasses on a tray. "Another beer for you guys?"

"Yeah, thanks, Angie," Simon said.

"Oh, and that's absinthe, so . . ." The waitress winked at Rikki. "Enjoy."

"The guy's ballsy sending a drink to you when you're clearly with us," Carter said.

"No, Mel is my roommate. He didn't bring a gift, so he said he'd buy me a drink." Then she frowned and stared at Carter. "What do you mean I'm clearly with you? I hope I haven't given you the wrong impression, but I don't go home with men I've just met."

"I didn't mean that," Carter said.

That was a lie and they all knew it. She picked up the shot and tipped it back, swallowing it in one gulp as she had the previous one. It was cool and refreshing, with a definite flavor of anise.

"Yes, you did. Or you were hoping."

"Rikki," Simon chimed in, "of course we were hoping. You're gorgeous. I noticed you as soon as you walked in. But we don't expect anything. Still, a man can hope." He gave her a crooked grin.

She liked Simon. And, God, he was hot. Her gaze drifted to Carter. He was, too.

Simon had dark brown hair, cut very short. She could imagine running her fingers over his scalp and feeling the bristles against her skin. His face was clean shaven and she could see a jagged scar along his neck, disappearing under the collar of his shirt. She wondered if he was ever in the military. He seemed used to being in charge.

Carter's sable brown hair was longer, but not a lot. Enough for it to coil into soft waves that she'd love to run her fingers through. His jaw sported bristly whiskers and a tattoo of a green vine with red roses coiled down his arm. He seemed more carefree than Simon. Willing to slide past a few rules if it suited him.

And their eyes. Carter's were an unusual amber, reminding her of a sunny day, though she could imagine them glowing like hot embers if he was aroused, while Simon's were the rich blue of a sapphire.

How had she wound up in a bar sitting with the two most gorgeous men in the place? Hell, they were the two most gorgeous men she'd ever seen before.

And they thought *she* was attractive.

So maybe she'd never been with a man before. That didn't mean she couldn't be with two.

Her first time with two men.

Her *first* time. With *two* men. She giggled.

That would be different. How many women could say they'd done that?

"I liked that last shot. I think I'll get another," she said.

"I'm not sure you should. Absinthe is pretty strong stuff," Simon said.

"Well, then how about we dance," she said. "I like to dance."

Simon stood up and waited while she stood. She slid her hand into his as they walked to the floor. He tightened his fingers around hers, sending a jolt of electricity through her.

Oh, God, she really couldn't shake this overwhelming sense that they were meant to be together. Their chemistry was off the charts.

Once on the dance floor, she slid her arms around his neck. It wasn't a slow song, but it wasn't too fast either. He guided her around the floor and she found herself moving closer to him. His arm slid around her waist and he drew her against his body.

His big, hard, muscular body.

Her body rippled with awareness. She could imagine him tilting up her face and claiming her lips, his large hand gliding up her back. Pulling her even tighter against him. She tilted her head and their gazes met. His sapphire blue eyes gleamed with interest and she could tell he wanted to kiss her as much as she wanted him to.

So she pushed herself onto her tiptoes and found his lips.

He groaned and pulled her tighter to him. His body seemed to envelop her, making her feel safe and cared for. His tongue dipped into her mouth and she started, then opened wide for him as he plunged in deep.

When he drew his mouth away, her eyes widened in surprise, then she realized the song had ended and people were moving past them as the band announced they'd be back after a short break. Simon curled his arm around her waist and guided her back to the table.

When they arrived, she sat down beside Carter. The waitress was passing by and Rikki asked her to bring another of the frosty drinks.

"You two seemed to enjoy your dance," Carter said.

Was he jealous?

"It was nice," she said, a little self-consciously.

She was a bit embarrassed that she'd kissed Simon—especially so publicly—but it had been phenomenally exciting.

She watched Carter as he tipped his beer back. What would it be like to kiss him?

And what the hell had happened to her inhibitions?

Her drink arrived and she took a deep sip. It was so sweet and fruity. And refreshingly cold. She took another sip.

Music started to play and she realized there was a DJ filling in while the band was on break. She turned to Carter.

"I like this song," she said, hoping he'd take the hint.

"Would you like to dance?" Carter asked.

She nodded and stood up, then took his hand as they walked together to the floor.

It was a slow song, so she stepped close and rested her hands on his shoulders as he slid his arms around her waist. The feel of his body so close as they moved to the music lit a fire inside her. She found herself melting against him, resting her head on his shoulder. His hand glided up her back and he stroked her neck under her hair, sending tingles dancing along her spine.

She seemed to float around the floor, enjoying the closeness of this strong, delectable man. At the heat swelling through her . . . the intense need gripping her . . . she wondered why she had resisted being with a man before. The answer, of course, was because she'd never felt this kind of heat before. This kind of feeling *just right*.

Except with Jesse.

So the real question was, why would she resist being with *this* man tonight? Going home with him and falling into his bed?

She nuzzled her lips against his neck and he turned to her, heat in his amber eyes. His lips moved to hers and their soft but persistent movement triggered a need so deep she thought she'd burst. She pressed her tongue to his lips and he opened, allowing her to glide inside. The bitter taste of beer only enhanced the sweetness of his tongue gliding over hers.

Her arms curled round his neck and she pulled him closer. Their legs still moved them around the floor, but she wanted him to sweep her off her feet and carry her to his car, then take her home and . . . *take* her.

His mouth parted from hers, but his eyes, gleaming with the same need she felt, remained locked on her.

"Let's go back to the table." His voice was a low rumble.

She nodded, then followed him as he led her from the floor, their fingers entwined.

As soon as she saw Simon at the table watching them, she broke out of the daze. Carter sat down across from Simon this time and she sat beside him. He pulled her close to his body, his arm gliding around her. Simon's gaze was fixed on her from across the table.

She drew in a deep breath.

"I . . . uh . . . I've never done this sort of thing before," she said. "How did you expect things would go? With the two of you, I mean."

Her head felt fuzzy and she really wasn't sure how to resolve this dilemma.

"Am I supposed to choose?" she asked.

Carter tightened his arm around her. "If you prefer one of us over the other, just tell us."

"If you don't want to do that," Simon said, "we could decide for you."

She bit her lip, knowing she didn't want that choice to be made at all.

"What if I want to go with both of you?"

Chapter Three

Fuck! Carter couldn't believe it. This soft, beautiful woman who had totally bewitched him with her smile . . . who had taken his breath away with her kiss . . . was suggesting that she be with both him and Simon.

He'd told Simon at the bar that it was the quiet ones who would surprise you, but when they'd actually met her, he was sure she'd never go for being with even one of them, let alone both.

His heart thundered in anticipation.

He glanced at Simon, seeing his own surprise reflected in his friend's eyes.

"We can go back to our place," Carter said, anxious to get her alone.

"You two share an apartment?"

"We live in a house about ten minutes from here," Simon answered.

She grabbed her drink, which was half full, and sipped through the straw. Then kept on drinking until it was gone.

Simon's gaze caught on Carter's and Carter just knew Simon was going to ruin this. Yeah, she'd had a few drinks, but nothing excessive. Enough to relax her, but not to impair her judgment.

He'd never been so hot for a woman. And he really believed she wanted them just as much, alcohol or no alcohol.

She smiled. "Let's go."

She stood up, purse in hand, and Carter surged after her, avoiding Simon's gaze. Carter took her hand and led her to the door. As soon as they were outside in the clear night air, Simon fell into step beside him.

"We should talk about this," Simon said under his breath, just loud enough for Carter to hear.

They turned the corner and Carter opened the passenger door for Rikki. Carter got into the driver's seat, leaving Simon to get in the back. Simon settled into the seat, giving Carter a sharp gaze in the rearview mirror.

As Carter started the car, Simon turned to Rikki.

"What's your address, Rikki?" Simon asked.

She turned to look at him. "I thought I was going home with you."

"I think it would be better if we took you home," Simon said.

"I thought you found me attractive." Uncertainty rippled through her voice.

"I do," Simon said. "We both do. But you've had a lot to drink."

She shook her head. "I've never done this before and . . . I know with you two it will be special."

Something niggled at Carter's gut. He knew she meant that she'd never gone home with someone she'd met at a bar before, but something about the way she said it made him wonder if . . .

Then he shook his head. No, there's no way she was a virgin. If she was, she certainly wouldn't go home with one of them, on the first night, let alone both of them.

Simon stared at him in the mirror from the backseat as Carter took the turn off the main street to Glendale. Five minutes later, he pulled into their driveway.

As they got out of the car, Simon shot him a glance that said nothing was going to happen tonight.

Once inside the house, Simon set her gift bag on the kitchen table.

"What did your friends get you as a gift?" Simon asked as he started to make coffee.

Rikki sat down at the table and pulled something out of the bag and unwrapped it.

"How did that cake survive the bag?" Carter asked as he sat down beside her, wishing she was in his arms instead.

"It's not really cake. It's soap."

"No shit?" He picked it up, then sniffed it. It smelled sweet. Like strawberries.

"Look, I know you two are trying to protect me because you think I've had too much to drink, but even before . . . when I first saw you at the bar . . . I was attracted to you. I might not have done this before, but I have a strong feeling. That it will be great."

"I'm *sure* it'll be great," Carter said.

"So I knew I wanted to be with you before I had the drinks and the alcohol just helped me see it more clearly."

"That's not how alcohol works," Simon said. "It *clouds* your judgment. It doesn't give you clarity."

She rested her hand on Simon's arm. "You don't get it. I knew I wanted to be with you the moment I saw you. But I was reluctant because I've never . . . well, I've already told you that. But I want to do this."

"Sweetheart, if you want to do this," Simon said, "then we can do it tomorrow. Or next week. There's no rush. Especially if it's right."

She frowned, and Carter was sure Simon had convinced her.

Damn it.

But he was right.

She reached for her purse and Carter figured she'd suggest they drive her home now.

"The soap was from one of my roommates. The other one, Tina, gave me something else."

She reached in her bag and pulled out a small, metal, mesh change purse, which she opened. Then she tugged out some black cloth. She laid it on the table and . . .

Damn. Carter's cock twitched. It was a thong. A sexy, almost not there, lacy thong.

She slid her hand inside and pushed against the inside of the crotch. One pink finger pushed through.

"See. They're crotchless."

"Fuck." Carter could just imagine her sweet little pussy inside there. And his cock, like her finger, pushing through the opening in the lace. The tip brushing against her slick flesh.

"Easy," Simon murmured. "We have to be strong."

Carter clenched his fists and breathed, trying to calm the dire need flooding through him.

"Fuck, Rikki, Simon is right. We can do this another night."

She frowned. "Oh."

She looked so dejected.

He couldn't help himself. He took her hand and brushed it over the hard bulge of his swollen cock. She gasped, her gaze darting to his.

"It's not that we don't want you. Desperately." He drew her hand away. "But it wouldn't be right."

She sighed. Her eyes were wide and dewy. "I was right. You two are very special."

"Come on. I'll drive you home," Simon said.

"I don't really feel like going home yet. Maybe I could have some of that coffee you're making. We could talk or watch a movie or something."

Carter glanced at Simon.

"Yeah, sure. A movie would be nice."

Simon didn't want to move. Rikki had fallen asleep during the movie and had snuggled up close to him, her soft curves pressing against him, making his groin ache with need.

He and Carter could have both fucked her tonight—she'd made it clear she wanted to—and he had longed to glide deep and hard into her soft, delightful body. But it wouldn't have been right. Her decision to go home with them hadn't happened until after she'd clearly been affected by the alcohol and was a direct contradiction to what she'd said earlier, so he had to respect her original attitude.

As difficult as it was after experiencing her soft lips and the willing gleam of desire in her eyes.

But now, with her warm body nestled against him, his willpower was waning.

"I think she should stay over." Carter sat on the other side of Rikki.

"We can't take advantage of her."

"I'm talking about putting her in the guest room." Carter scooped her up and carried her down the hall.

Simon hurried ahead and slipped into his bedroom to grab a T-shirt, then followed Simon into the guest room. He pulled back the duvet so Simon could lay her on the sheet.

Carter leaned in close to her. "Rikki?"

"Hmm," she grumbled sleepily.

"You can stay here tonight if you like."

She opened her eyes halfway. "Tired," she mumbled.

"It's okay," Simon said. "You can just fall asleep. But here's a T-shirt for you to change into so you'll be more comfortable."

She sat up and took the T-shirt from him, then reached around behind her to unzip her dress.

"Can't reach."

Carter glanced at Simon and Simon shrugged, so Carter unfastened the zipper for her. She pushed the dress down, revealing a cotton-candy pink satin bra with off-white lace trim, then wiggled out of the dress and tossed it to the foot of the bed.

"She seems to have this under control," Carter said.

When Simon saw her reaching behind her back to unhook her bra—fuck, then start to pull it off—he grabbed Carter's arm.

"Let's leave her to it," Simon said, steadfastly directing his gaze to the door.

"You sure?" Carter asked, resisting the pull of Simon's arm as Simon propelled them from the room.

"I'm a lot more sure now than I will be if we stay ten more seconds," Simon answered.

When he reached the door, as much as he tried to resist, his head pivoted back to glance at her. Luckily for his peace of mind, she was pulling the T-shirt down past her waist. But as he reached for the light switch, he couldn't help noticing the outline of her nipples showing through the thin fabric.

Fuck, she was either very cold or very turned on.

His cock swelled and he had an almost uncontrollable urge to head right back to the bed and find out which.

Rikki blinked, sunlight dazzling through the light curtains on the window. She sat up and glanced around, uncertainty gripping her.

This wasn't her room.

Where was she?

Then the memories came crashing back. She'd met two guys—two hot, incredibly sexy men—at the bar last night. And . . .

Oh, God, she'd practically thrown herself at them.

She didn't remember everything, but they had . . .

She ran her fingers through her hair.

They'd turned her down. Because she'd been drunk.

Her cheeks heated in embarrassment.

At least they were honorable. They had refused to take advantage of her in that state. She remembered Simon insisting on taking her to her own home.

She glanced around again. Yet here she was.

There was no man in the bed, but maybe one of them—or both—had taken her up on her offer. A dim memory of watching a movie and then being carried in here flickered through her brain. Then Simon giving her a T-shirt and . . . Her cheeks burned hotter. She had stripped off her dress right in front of them. Then her bra.

She remembered the heat in Simon's eyes as he'd stood at the door staring at her, clearly fighting his urges.

If only she could remember what had happened next.

She flung her arm over her eyes. Just her luck to lose her virginity to one . . . or maybe two . . . handsome, sexy men . . . and not even be able to remember it!

A knock sounded at the door. She grabbed the covers and pulled them tight to her body.

"What is it?" she called out.

"Rikki, it's Simon. Sorry to wake you but you've gotten a few text messages on your phone. The last one was from someone named Cassie hoping to meet you in an hour. I thought it might be important."

She sat up. "Come in."

The door opened and Simon stepped into the room. He wore pajama bottoms, but no top and—her heart stuttered in her chest—his body was magnificent. Every inch from his slim waist to his broad shoulders was tight sculpted muscles. There was a jagged scar starting at his neck and extending partway down his chest, but it only added to his masculine aura.

He walked to the bed and held out her cell phone, the shifting pastel mint and pink glitters in the liquid case shimmering in the sunlight.

She pulled up the string of texts that started about two hours ago. Cassie said she'd been able to set up a meeting at the firehouse and she wanted Rikki to meet her there at eleven o'clock. She sent a few more texts, the last one asking if she could meet her at the Starbucks on Wilchester and Brook Streets, which Rikki knew was a block from the firehouse.

She bit her lip. How would she get there in time?

"My friend Cassie wants me to meet her. It's about a project we're working on together."

"If you need a ride, Carter and I can drive you. We have to go out anyway."

"Thank you. That would be a real help, but I'm afraid I have to stop at my place first. I don't want to make you late."

She needed to change into something more business-like and pick up her camera.

"No problem. There's a shower in the bathroom to the left down the hallway."

"Thanks."

As Simon headed to the door, she sucked in a breath. "Simon?"

He stopped and turned.

"Last night . . . did you and I . . . or Carter and I . . ." She bit her lip. "Did anything happen?"

His eyebrow arched. "You don't remember?"

She shook her head, her stomach quivering.

"No, nothing happened last night. We resisted your seductive powers." His lips turned up in a devilish grin and his eyes glittered. "But now that we know how attracted you are to us . . . and that you're interested in being with both of us"—his smile widened—"we plan to take you up on your offer as soon as possible."

Rikki got out of the car and waved good-bye to Simon and Carter, then went into the Starbucks. Cassie was waiting at a table with two lattes. Rikki sat down and Cassie pushed one in front of her.

"Morning," Cassie said. "I'm glad you could make it. I know it's short notice, but the fire chief, Lou, who's a friend of mine, suggested we work with one specific crew for the photos. These guys work twenty-four-hour shifts followed by forty-eight hours off and he wants you to come in and meet the two lieutenants today so you can talk about ideas for the calendar, then get started tomorrow when they're on duty."

"So these guys are coming in on their day off?"

"That's right. They think it'll be a fun project and are looking forward to meeting you." Cassie sipped her coffee. "Tomorrow, they can take you through their day and help you get a feel for the firehouse and the equipment so you can plan what pictures you want to take and what equipment and props you might want to use."

"All right. Well, let's get going."

"Wait a minute." Cassie grinned. "First, tell me how it went last night. And who those two guys were who just dropped you off."

"Oh. I met them at the bar last night."

Cassie's eyes widened. "And you spent the night with them? *Both* of them?"

"Yes, but not what you think. I accidentally had too much to drink—"

"Accidentally?"

"—and they were perfect gentlemen."

"Even though you went home with them?"

"They realized I was a little drunk and backed off."

"So now that you're stone cold sober, how do you feel about them?"

Rikki stared at the white cap on her latte cup and smiled. "I gave them my number. I think I'd like to see where things might go."

Cassie laughed, her blue eyes sparkling. "That's great." She shook her head, a bright grin on her face. "I never would have thought you'd even consider being with two men." She glanced at her watch. "Okay, *now* we really do have to get going."

Rikki followed Cassie into the building. The firehouse was a delightful structure—a two-story brick building with large curved windows on the upper floor that probably gave fantastic lighting up there. There were large windows on the main floor, too, even on the big red garage doors.

Inside was spacious and it was well lit with the morning light, just as she'd anticipated. There were two big fire trucks, lots of equipment, and several fire poles. And big men moving about the place, mostly checking the equipment.

"Cassie, nice to see you." A tall man with a salt and pepper beard walked their way, a big smile on his face.

"Good morning. Rikki, this is Chief Lou Anderson. Chief, this is Rikki. She's the photographer I was telling you about."

He wrapped his big hand around Rikki's and shook it. "Nice to meet you, Rikki. I heard you just moved here from Ohio. How do you like our little town so far?"

"It's very nice. I think I'll like living here."

He laughed, deep in his belly. "You'd find it hard not to love Muldone. I've lived here all my life and I can't imagine living anywhere else." He released her hand, then turned and started walking. "Come on back to my office and we'll discuss the project."

Rikki trailed after Cassie as they walked through the firehouse, getting a few glances from the firefighters. Of course, with the sway of Cassie's hips in her tight pencil skirt, Rikki wasn't surprised. Cassie oozed sophistication and sex appeal. Her long blonde hair was coiled and clipped up, and her suit jacket hugged her slim waist.

Rikki wore a pair of dress pants and a royal blue silk blouse. She didn't have a lot of business clothes, since the store she'd worked in had required they wear casual, trendy clothes. Basically, she had this one pair of dress pants and a couple of blouses to wear with them.

The chief opened a door and led them into a large office with a desk and a rectangular table with six wheeled chairs around it.

"Sit." He gestured to the table, so Rikki sat down in the chair next to Cassie. "I called in my two lieutenants on the shift you'll be working with. They should be here any minute. Would you like some coffee?"

At their polite nods, he grabbed the thermos jug on the table and filled two empty mugs, then handed one to Cassie and one to Rikki.

Rikki added some cream from the little metal jug on the table and added a pouch of sugar. Through the glass window looking into the rest of the firehouse, she could see the big strapping men moving around, sending her the occasional curious glances. She wondered what they thought of her. Her stomach quivered. She wondered how she'd handle watching them strip off their shirts, revealing their muscular bodies, then trying to direct these huge, authoritative figures as she shot the photos.

The thought reminded her of Simon this morning when she'd seen him without his shirt, his muscular chest so sinfully masculine. Knocking her totally off balance.

A knock sounded at the door.

"Come in," the chief called.

The door opened and two men stepped inside.

Rikki's eyes widened and her heart stammered.

Oh, God. It couldn't be.

Chapter Four

Carter and Simon had gotten a call this morning asking if they'd come into the firehouse to meet the photographer who'd be working on the calendar. Carter didn't mind stopping in on his day off, especially for this project, which he thought would be a lot of fun . . . and would raise money for some worthwhile causes around the neighborhood.

He might have resented being called in if Rikki hadn't been called away, too. He wouldn't have minded trying to convince her to move forward from where they'd left things at the bar. The thought of those tiny crotchless panties in her purse still had him hot and throbbing.

But they'd dropped her off to meet her friend and then driven here. They'd spent a few minutes chatting to a couple of the other men in the parking lot before they came in.

When they walked into the chief's office, he saw that the chief was sitting at the table with two women. He knew Cassie already and sent her a smile. Then his gaze fell on the other woman.

As soon as he saw her auburn hair and lovely heart-shaped face, his lips turned up in a broader smile.

It was Rikki.

Her eyes widened when she saw them, then turned glacial as she dropped her gaze to her coffee. The same look he'd seen her give the men who'd approached her table at Rango's to send them away.

What the fuck?

"Rikki," the chief said, "this is Lieutenant Simon Davies and Lieutenant Carter Fenn."

"Actually, we've already met," Simon said. "Hi, Rikki."

Cassie nudged Rikki and she tipped her face up again. "Yes, hi."

Carter sat in the chair beside Rikki and Simon at the next chair, which was at the end of the table, across from the chief.

The chief recapped the plan they'd already discussed about the photographer—Rikki—joining them for their shift tomorrow and showing her around.

"Whatever access you need to the men and the firehouse and equipment, just let me know and we'll make it work."

"Thank you, Chief. We appreciate that," Cassie said.

"Yes. Thank you, Chief," Rikki added.

Carter watched her, wondering why she was so subdued. And why she refused to make eye contact with them. Was she afraid they'd embarrass her because of last night? Did she think they'd brag to their buddies about how they'd taken her home? Insinuating they'd fucked her?

"Okay, I've got to get back to work," the chief said. "Why don't you two take the ladies to lunch and discuss what Rikki has in mind? You might want to brainstorm with some ideas of your own, too. Now's the time." The chief stood up and the others followed his lead.

"Cassie, why don't you and Rikki come in our car?" Simon suggested.

Cassie smiled. "That would be lovely. Thanks." Cassie grabbed Rikki's arm and led her after them.

"Knightley's?" Carter suggested.

"Perfect," Cassie answered.

When they got to the car, Carter opened the back door and Cassie got in while Rikki got in the other door that Simon had opened for her, mumbling her thanks. Simon sent him a questioning stare over the roof of the car as they closed the doors, clearly as perplexed by Rikki's cold shoulder as Carter was.

Rikki tried to avoid Cassie's inquiring glance as the men got into the car. They drove to the restaurant and as soon as they were at the table, Cassie grabbed her arm.

"Let's go to the ladies' room," Cassie said. "Guys, could you order us a couple of diet colas?"

As soon as Cassie ushered Rikki into the bathroom, Cassie turned to her.

"I didn't know it was Simon and Carter you were with last night."

If Cassie hadn't been able to tell by her reaction in the chief's office, she would have figured it out when they got

into the same car she'd seen Rikki get out of at the Starbucks.

"So what gives?" Cassie asked. "You said you'd like to
see where things go with them, but now you're treating
them like you're the ice queen."

"Why does everyone keep saying that?" Rikki asked.
"I'm just not being overly friendly."

"Rikki, you look like you're a porcupine with icicle
quills. But whatever. Why are you freezing them out?"

Rikki frowned. "You know why. Because they're firefighters."

"You don't have to marry them. Just open up a little
more. Get to know them. See where it leads."

Rikki shook her head. "I don't think I can. I . . ." She
shrugged. "I don't think I can just have a casual relationship of any kind with them. I think . . . I mean, if I do, I
might . . ."

"You might what?"

Rikki sighed.

"When I met them . . . I got a feeling about them."

"What kind of feeling?"

Rikki shifted. "The same kind of feeling I had with
Jesse when I met him."

"Oh, honey . . ." Cassie pulled her into a hug and
stroked her hair. When she pulled back, she smiled. "Maybe
you think it's the same feeling because . . . well, because
you're really hot for these guys and your subconscious is
trying to push you past your block against being with a
firefighter."

"And getting hurt."

"Did you actually get this feeling for both of them?"

Rikki nodded.

"Well, there, you see? That doesn't make sense. You're not going to fall in love with two men at the same time. So my advice is that you *hang out*"—she winked—"with both of them, and see what happens. And if you're always with both of them, you won't make a really deep connection with either of them."

Rikki's heart clenched, remembering the pain of losing Jesse. Remembering the strength of the feeling she'd had when she saw Simon and Carter.

"I don't think so," Rikki said.

When Rikki and Cassie got back to the table, the guys already had the drinks. Seconds after they sat down to look at the menus, the waitress brought a plate of nachos.

After they ordered, the four of them talked about the calendar shoot. Rikki said she'd bring her equipment the next day and set up in the firehouse. She'd take some sample pictures in various locations to see what worked best with lighting and background. She asked if there was a space she could set up her computer for reviewing photos and Simon told her they could provide her with some desk space.

After lunch, she pulled out her tablet and showed them some research she'd done—other calendars of firefighters—and asked what kind of thing they were going for. Some had flames Photoshopped into the images, blazing around the men, or behind them. Some had the firefighters posing with equipment or ladders. Most had the men in their thick uniform pants with suspenders over their bare chests.

"I think we should go sexier," Cassie said, as she swiped through the photos. "Maybe ditch the big pants and suspenders and have them in tight shorts or maybe just boxers, holding their hats or hoses." She chuckled to herself. "Their *fire* hoses of course."

Carter's eyebrow shot up. "You want us to be boy toys?"

"Well, yeah," Cassie shot back with a grin. "That's why women are buying these calendars. Sex sells, right? So let's make them as sexy as possible. All the profits go to charity, so let's try to make this as sellable as we can."

"What do you think, Rikki?" Simon asked, his gaze locking on her in a most disturbing fashion.

She shifted on the wooden bench. "I . . . uh . . . yeah, well, Cassie knows more about marketing than I do."

"So you think we should strip down to our boxers for you." Carter winked. "I mean . . . for the calendar."

She felt her cheeks flush.

"That would be great for the romance cover shots, too," Cassie said. "You can really push the limits with those ones." She grinned. "The sexier the better."

"Are you suggesting we pose naked?" Simon asked, a glint in his eye. "I mean, not that I'd mind posing that way for you, Rikki. I just don't know about having a naked photo of me going public."

Cassie grinned. "I'm sure Rikki will ensure it's tastefully cropped."

"I think Rikki could take a few with just Simon and

me," Carter suggested. "Just so we can see how she handles it."

"*Handles* what?" Cassie asked with an innocent look on her face.

Oh, God. Rikki's cheeks flushed even hotter, and she jabbed Cassie in the ribs.

Startled, Cassie glanced her way and at the sharp gaze Rikki sent her, Cassie looked abashed.

"Uh, sorry, Rikki. Guys, I shouldn't have been kidding around like that. I'm embarrassing Rikki."

Simon's somber gaze shifted to hers. "Sorry if our kidding embarrassed you, Rikki. No one's going to push anything you're uncomfortable with."

Staring into his reassuring blue eyes, she knew he meant more than the types of pictures they were talking about.

She nodded. "Thank you."

"And if any of the guys get rowdy or do something they don't realize is making you uncomfortable, just let Carter or me know. Okay?"

She stared down at her empty plate and nodded.

Damn, why did he have to be so nice? The way he was being protective of her made her heart swell and her body quiver.

She wanted to be in his arms.

But she couldn't let that happen.

To Rikki lunch seemed interminable. Finally, the bill came and she finished her last sip of coffee as Simon paid for all of them.

Cassie glanced at her watch. "Oh, crap. I didn't realize

it was so late. I have to meet a client in fifteen minutes. Simon, do you think you could drive Rikki home after you drop me off?"

"Our pleasure," Simon answered.

Rikki sent Cassie a sharp glance.

"Sorry, hon. But I know Simon and Carter will take good care of you."

Rikki bit back the response she was going to make, that she could just walk home. Or Uber.

But she realized she needed to face them alone sometime. It wasn't fair to just turn off her plans to see them again with no explanation.

They walked to the car and Simon got in the driver's seat. Ten minutes later he let Cassie out at the parking lot behind the Starbucks near the firehouse. As soon as they pulled away from the curb, Carter turned to her in the backseat.

"You were surprised to see us at the firehouse this morning."

She glanced down at her hands. "That's true."

"You seemed really uncomfortable. If you don't want the other guys to know what's going on between us, we won't tell them."

If the other firefighters knew she was having hot sex with both these men—which is probably where things would have gone—she *would* be embarrassed. But that wasn't going to happen now.

She held her silence and Carter frowned.

"Is there something else wrong?" he asked.

She pursed her lips. "Yes, but . . ." She drew in a breath.

She didn't want to talk about it in a quick conversation in the car. They deserved better than that. "Look, when we get to my place, why don't you come in for a coffee?"

When they pulled into the parking space in front of the townhouse, Carter got out and opened her door. They went inside and she kicked off her shoes.

"Are your roommates here?" Simon asked.

He and Carter filled the small entryway with their tall, broad-shouldered frames.

"They're all at work."

Simon smiled and glided his hands over her shoulders, then drew her to him. As his lips moved to hers for a kiss, she ducked away, slipping from his embrace.

She led them into the kitchen, then put on a pot of coffee. They all sat on the stools at the counter.

"I know we really hit it off last night and we clearly share a mutual attraction . . ." She frowned. She didn't want to have this conversation. The pain was already gripping her heart.

"You're not going to tell us you don't want to pursue that attraction, are you?" Simon said. "We have a real chemistry. It would be a shame not to see where it might lead."

She shook her head. "That's the thing. I don't want it to lead anywhere."

"Is it because of the idea of having a threesome?" Simon asked. "Because if that's it, we can back off on that."

"That's not it. I mean, it's not like I've ever done something like that before, but I'm equally attracted to both of you. And the thought of . . ." Goose bumps quivered up her arms. "Well, it would be very exciting. But that's not it."

She poured three cups of coffee and placed one in front of each of them, then sipped her own.

"This isn't easy to say, but the reason I don't want to be with you is . . . because you're firefighters." She gazed at them, praying for them to understand. "It's not that I don't respect what you do. I think it's noble and very courageous. I admire you for it."

She stared down at her cup.

"But . . ."

She sucked in a trembling breath, feeling her emotions get the better of her.

Simon could see the anxiety and sadness in Rikki's eyes. He and Carter exchanged a glance.

"Tell us, Rikki," Carter prompted when she continued to hesitate.

"I dated a firefighter a long time ago."

"Did he break your heart?" Carter asked.

She shook her head.

Fuck. Simon knew exactly where this was heading.

"What happened, Rikki?" Simon asked softly.

"He . . ." But her voice cracked before she got too far and she covered her mouth.

He could see the sheen in her eyes. He stood up and stepped close to her, then drew her into his arms. He could feel the wetness on his shirt as her tears escaped. She sucked in a breath and shook her head, then drew back.

"He died and . . . I was shattered. He was everything to me. I was really young, but we knew we were meant to be together. We were going to be married. Then . . ." She gazed up at him, the depth of grief in her eyes so intense it tore at his heart.

He grasped her shoulders, capturing her gaze. "It is a dangerous profession, it's true. But you can't live your life in fear."

"I agree. That's why I won't get involved with a fire-fighter again."

"That's not what I meant."

Her gaze dropped and he cupped her chin and tipped it up so she was looking at him again.

"You need to take risks or life isn't worth living."

"Spoken like a true firefighter." Her words were a mere whisper.

His jaw clenched. He'd be damned if he was going to give up on her, despite her fear.

He drew her into his arms again, savoring the sweetness of her soft body against his and captured her lips. She stiffened, her hands flattening against his chest. But as his tongue nudged its way into her mouth, finding the sweetness inside, the pressure of her palms against him eased and her hands glided to his shoulders. Soon she was clinging to him, her lips moving with his.

Then he drew back, his arms still around her.

"Can you really ignore the heat between us?"

"I have to. For my own sanity."

But the doubt in her eyes gave him renewed hope.

He sat back down and sipped his coffee, then gazed around.

"You know, after we dropped you off, Carter mentioned that there've been problems with these rental properties before."

"That's right," Carter said. "The company that manages them isn't as diligent as it should be when it comes to fire safety. There's been at least one fire because of faulty or poorly maintained wiring."

"Since we're here," Simon said, "would you let us check out the smoke alarms?"

"I don't know."

"I don't mean to make trouble for your landlord. We won't put in an official report or anything," Simon said. "We just want to make sure you're safe."

"I guess that would be all right. As long as you don't go into my roommates' bedrooms. It wouldn't be right to invade their privacy."

"Can we go into *your* bedroom?" Carter asked.

Chapter Five

The thought of the wiring being unsafe made Rikki a little nervous.

"Yes, of course." But then the smile that crept across the men's faces made her cheeks flush. "Oh, I didn't mean . . ."

Simon chuckled. "Yeah, we know."

"Do you have a stepladder and a screwdriver?" Carter asked as he stood up.

"I'm not sure. We do have a step stool for reaching the top cabinets." She walked to the window where the plastic step stool sat with a large green spider plant on top of it and moved the plant to the counter. It was just a utility stool with two steps on the side.

"That'll do," Carter said as he took it from her and set it under the smoke detector in the kitchen.

She watched as Carter stepped to the top of it and marveled that it could hold his large body. He reached the smoke detector with no problem at all. He fiddled with it, then turned to Simon and shook his head.

He climbed down again and picked up the stool, then the two of them disappeared out of the room. Over the next half hour, they checked every one of the devices. When they finally went up to the third floor where her bedroom was, she opened the door for them.

As they glanced around her small bedroom, their big masculine bodies filling her private space, their gazes perusing the feminine decor—floral print curtains and bedding, silk flowers, frills on her throw cushions, et cetera—she felt very exposed.

After Carter finished checking the smoke detector and got down from the stool, his arm bumped against her. She glanced up at him and heat flashed through his eyes, then his gaze wandered to her bed.

She tensed, ignoring the fluttery feeling in her stomach, as she moved toward the door.

"So are you finished?"

"Yes. At least three of them need to be replaced," Carter said.

"I'd recommend replacing them all, just to be on the safe side," Simon said.

"Will that be very expensive?" she asked. She didn't have much left in her savings.

"Don't worry about it," Carter said. "We'll replace them for you."

"I can't let you do that. I should just go to the landlord."

"With this company, that'll take forever, and they'll probably put in something substandard. Don't worry about it," Simon said. "We get a great discount on smoke detectors. And how would it look if the house where the official

Opal Carew

photographer for our calendar lived burned down? We have to protect the reputation of the department."

Simon turned to Carter. "I'll go turn off the breakers so you can take down the units while I go buy some new ones."

"Sure thing." Carter grabbed the stool and the two of them headed down the stairs, Rikki trailing behind them.

Two hours later, Tina walked in to see Carter on the step stool in the living room busily working at replacing the device while Simon was working on the one in the kitchen, standing on a small stepladder he'd grabbed from his house when he'd gone shopping to pick up the new smoke detectors.

"What's going on?" Tina asked.

Her pointed nails were adorned with a metallic foil that transitioned from red to purple to blue with round silver studs polka-dotting her ring fingers. Her skirt was short and her V-neck plunging. As usual.

"Tina, this is Simon and Carter."

Carter glanced at her and smiled. "Nice to meet you."

Simon waved from the kitchen.

"They're firemen from the station where I'm doing the calendar shoot. They drove me home and noticed a problem with the smoke detectors."

"Yeah? Nice to meet you." Tina lowered her voice. "They were also the guys you left with last night." She nudged Rikki and sent her a wink. "Bravo, by the way."

Tina's gaze raked down Carter's body and settled on his crotch, as if evaluating. Then she pulled Rikki up the stairs with her to the second floor.

"You know, I see these sexy guys doing a lot of screwing. Maybe you should give them a *hand,* you know what I mean?"

Rikki laughed, then started down the stairs again, but Tina gripped her arm, stopping her.

"Seriously though," Tina said. "Did anything happen last night? And more importantly, is either of them available?"

"Down, girl. Nothing happened, and I can't play matchmaker. I have to work with these guys. I don't want it to get complicated."

Tina frowned. "Okay. But I think it's a real waste. Two hot firemen right here in my own house and I can't touch." She turned and headed up the next flight of stairs to the third floor where both of their bedrooms were. "See you later."

When Rikki returned to the main floor, Carter was sitting on the couch. Simon was finishing up in the kitchen.

"That roommate of yours is pretty cute," Carter said.

"I guess she is." Rikki pushed aside the jealousy surging through her at his interest.

"I think it's pretty interesting that you wouldn't try to set her up with either of us, especially since you say you don't want to get involved with us."

Oh, God, he'd actually heard them. She sat on the easy chair, her stomach clenching.

"Are you saying you want to get involved with Tina?" she asked.

"Well, we're not giving up on you," Carter said, his lips turning up in a smile. "But we've never had a problem sharing."

Rikki's cheeks heated at his provocative teasing.

Simon laughed, then winked at her.

"So we're all done here," Simon said. "Do you want to go see how effective the smoke detector is in your bedroom?"

Oh, God, with the way Simon was looking at her . . . the way they were both looking at her . . . with a blaze of heat in their eyes . . . she had to beat back the flame of her own arousal.

"Thanks very much for what you've done. I'll see you at the firehouse tomorrow."

The next morning, Carter and Simon picked Rikki up on the way to the firehouse. They'd insisted on giving her a ride so she wouldn't have to lug her equipment on public transit. She'd put it all in a wheeled suitcase, but it would have been awkward getting it on and off the bus.

Simon pulled the suitcase out of the trunk and rolled it toward the building as she walked by his side, her stomach fluttering a little at the idea of meeting the other men.

It was a hot day outside, so she was glad to step into the air-conditioned building. Simon led her to the living area where the men spent downtime and put her stuff by a desk in the corner near a big window.

"You can set up your computer here," he said. "I need to go do some things. I'll leave you in Carter's capable hands."

She nodded, her thoughts jumping to images of what she'd like his capable hands to be doing.

Carter took her through the station to show her around,

introducing her to the men as they went, while Simon disappeared to do whatever he had to do.

The men were all tall and broad shouldered and she felt a little intimidated by them, even though they were all very friendly. After they'd done the rounds, with Carter stopping along the way to explain various equipment, she couldn't remember which names belonged to which faces.

"So do you want to get started?" Carter asked as they returned to the living area. "I can help you set up your equipment."

"Actually, I was thinking maybe I'd take some pictures around the firehouse to get a sense of the lighting and what areas would work best for background. There's some great natural light in here with the big windows. But I think we probably want some of the pictures with props like an axe or fire hose."

Three men she hadn't met walked into the room. The tallest, at about six five, had close-cropped brown hair, electric blue eyes that locked on her like lasers. He wore a T-shirt and his arms were totally covered in tattoos. The man next to him had longer, sandy brown wavy hair with a crooked smile turning up his lips and a twinkle in his eyes. The third man seemed a little younger and gazed at her with curiosity and, she sensed, a little shyness. His thick, black hair had a casual, carelessly spiked look. She wasn't sure if it was because he'd styled it that way, or it had been mussed by wearing a cap, but she had the urge to stroke her fingers through it to smooth it into place.

"Heard tell that we missed the intros with the photographer," the sandy-haired man said with a Texas drawl. His gaze locked on her and his smile broadened. "I take it this pretty little lady is her."

Rikki felt her cheeks flush at his frank attention.

"I'm Rikki." She held out her hand to shake his.

He took it, but instead of wrapping it in a firm handshake, he brought it to his lips. The light brush of a kiss sent tingles dancing along her spine.

"Rikki, this guy is Tanner," Carter said, then pointed to the tattooed man. "That's Dodge, and Kyle's the short one."

The *short one* he referred to was at least six feet tall.

Dodge nodded, one side of his mouth turning up in a sexy, almost feral smile. Her insides quivered at the exciting, bad-boy vibe the man put out. She shook hands with him, and his big fingers squeezed firmly.

The strength of his grip made her feel soft and feminine in contrast. She felt a sense of power thrumming through him, and knew that when he was with a woman, he would be in total control. And as his gaze locked with hers, she felt an overwhelming desire to experience his commanding presence as he took charge of her.

When she turned to Kyle, he offered his hand and she shook it. His hold was lighter, as if he wanted to handle her with care, and he sent her a boyish grin. "Nice to meet you, ma'am."

"Thank you. Me, too," she said.

"I heard you talkin' about props for the pictures," Tanner said. "What about the fire truck?"

"Yes, I'd definitely like some pictures with the truck in the background."

"If you're takin' casual pictures, your timing's perfect. We're going out now to wash it."

Carter frowned. "Wasn't it just washed yesterday?"

Dodge grinned. "But it's hot out and we thought it would be a good way to cool off, and at the same time, give the lady an idea of some good actions shots." Although he was talking to Carter, his blue-eyed gaze remained locked on Rikki.

She drew in a deep, trembling breath as his words made her think of muscled firefighters, shirts off, her hands gliding over their hard, ridged bodies.

"I'll grab my camera so I can take pictures."

"No," Dodge said. "We thought you should help."

She glanced down at her dress pants and soft pink blouse. "I'm not really dressed for it."

Tanner laughed. "No problem, darlin'. Here you go." He tossed her the bag he had tucked under his arm.

She caught it and peered inside. It was a pair of navy shorts with the fire department patch and a white T-shirt.

"We wouldn't want you to get your pretty work clothes all wet."

His words melted through her and she could just imagine walking around the bright red truck in a skimpy bathing suit, the men watching her, sudsy water sloshing from a big bucket as she lifted a sponge and glided it over the shiny metal. Except that the truck became Simon, and as she stroked him, feeling every ridged contour of his body, slickness oozed between her legs.

She sucked in a breath, forcing herself back to the here and now.

"Actually, I think I'll be fine in what I'm wearing."

Carter leaned in and said, "Go ahead and put on our gear. It'll be a good way for you to bond with the guys. Become part of the team."

She pursed her lips as she took the shorts and top and nodded. "Yeah, okay."

"Come on. I'll show you where you can change," Carter said.

She followed Carter up the stairs to the second floor. She hadn't been to the private area of the firehouse yet and was surprised as she walked down a hallway to see bedrooms with two beds in each room. On the other side of the hallway, there were several large, closet-sized indents in the wall with fire poles to the lower floor.

"I thought you'd all sleep in one large room with lots of beds," she said.

"That's typical, but they've done studies on sleep issues with firefighters working around the clock and found that having a more private space allows better sleep. Our chief decided to give it a try and had the place renovated."

He led her to the end of the hall and up another stairway. The third floor was smaller than the one below and he led her down a short hallway.

"This is where Simon and I sleep. You can change in here."

They walked into a larger room than the ones for the other men. It was simple, with two double beds covered with plain navy comforters, a bedside table between them, and two desks, each by a window. There was also a dresser where they probably kept a change of clothes or two while they were on duty.

"Okay. Thanks."

He left the room, closing the door behind him and she dropped the garments on one of the beds and kicked off her shoes.

She unbuttoned her blouse and laid it over the back of the desk chair, then unfastened her pants. She was glad she wore one of her good bra and panty sets today. Light pink, so her bra didn't show through the white T-shirt too obviously.

Looking down at her bra, she imagined Carter walking into the room, then stepping behind her and cupping her breasts. She could almost feel his lips nuzzling the side of her neck as his fingers glided over her hardening nipples and squeezed them.

She sucked in a breath and shooed the images away.

Good lord, what's wrong with me lately?

She quickly pulled on the shorts, then the white T-shirt over top and tucked it in. She glanced at her shoes, but it didn't make sense to put on dress shoes while washing a truck, so she decided to go barefoot.

When she went down the stairs, the firehouse seemed empty. The big garage door was open and she saw sunlight glinting off the shiny red finish of the truck. She walked outside and saw all the men wearing navy shorts like the ones she had on and navy T-shirts, also with the fire department patch.

A few of the men whistled as she walked toward the truck.

"Over here, Rikki," Carter called. He and Simon were standing at the side of the truck with a couple of buckets of water. Rikki walked toward the men. Trying to play it cool even though being surrounded by so many gorgeous men made her knees weak.

As she glanced around at their grinning faces, she knew they were planning something, but she had no idea what.

Then in the blink of an eye, they all tugged down their shorts, exposing brief bathing suits beneath. Shorts flew through the air as they tossed them away. They all placed their hands on their hips, their chests puffed forward, looking like a team of Greek gods posing for her.

The bathing suits were compact and hugged their hips and groins. The shapes beneath those shorts were very distinctive. Not much was left to the imagination. She turned to Simon and Carter and realized they were also in fitted bathing suits. The thought of reaching out and stroking the packages hidden beneath the fabric became overwhelming.

Not that she'd do it here.

Oh, God, not that I'd do it at all.

"I think we've embarrassed the pretty little lady," Tanner observed, a hint of concern in his eyes.

Dodge chuckled, a deep rumble from his chest. "Lady, if you can't handle this, how are you going to handle taking sexy shots of us for the calendar? I was ready to strip all the way down if you wanted me to. It's for a good cause, right?" He smiled devilishly.

Dodge's arms were sleeved in tattoos and most of his torso was inked. He would make one sexy cover model. That was for sure. All she could think about when she looked at him was tracing the lines of his tattoos up his bulging biceps, over his shoulder, then down his chest . . . then his torso . . . and . . . Oh, God, she was staring at his crotch. And the fabric was being stretched tighter beneath her gaze as she watched.

Chapter Six

Knowing she had to hold her own with these men, Rikki dragged her gaze to his with bravado and pushed back her shoulders.

"I'm not embarrassed. Except for you guys, 'cause you're slacking off. This truck won't wash itself."

"Oh, burn!" Carter said.

She laughed and grabbed a sponge from the soapy bucket. "How about I race you to finish washing this thing?"

"But, baby," Dodge said. "It's not about speed. The best work is the kind that's done slow and with a lot of attention."

His suggestive tone sent heat skittering through her.

"You are so bad," she said, pushing back her embarrassment.

He winked at her. "And when I'm bad, I'm *very* good."

She dipped her sponge in the water, soaking it good, then flung it at Dodge. True to his name, he saw it coming and jerked to the side, so the sponge slammed against Tanner with a splat, suds flying.

Tanner laughed and grabbed the hose from his friend,

then soaked her with a cold spray of water. She gasped, then turned her back. The water stopped and she pushed her drenched hair from her face, finding herself giggling. Until she realized her pink bra was clearly visible through her T-shirt, and her nipples were so hard from the cold that they were nearly tearing through the fabric.

And Carter and Simon had definitely noticed. She could see their bathing suits stretching over their swelling shafts.

"You know, guys," she said as she crossed her arms over her chest as nonchalantly as she could. "I think you need to get to work. I'm going to go dry off and then get some candid shots. They'll be great for some of the promos Cassie wants to do for the calendar."

With that, she escaped to the firehouse with as much dignity as she could muster.

Rikki grabbed a towel from a pile someone had set on the couch and dried her skin as she walked up the stairs. She'd love a shower, and knew there would be one in the place, but she did not want to chance any of the men walking in on her, so she went straight back to the bedroom and closed the door, then stripped off the wet T-shirt and shorts.

She dried herself off and wrapped her hair in the towel, then peered out the window to see the men continuing to wash the truck below.

When she realized Carter was staring at her through the window, she dodged back. Of course, he wouldn't be able to see that she was just wearing her bra and panties from down there . . . not at that angle . . .

She hoped.

Her cheeks heated as she pulled on the rest of her clothes. She was already on the verge of being highly unprofessional. Putting on a peep show for her models would be over the line.

She went down the stairs and grabbed her camera. She told them she'd take photos of them washing the truck, so that's what she intended to do.

Rikki spent about twenty minutes snapping shots of the mostly naked men washing the big truck. She took a lot of candid shots, but also got them to do some casual poses. Finally, they trickled into the firehouse and got dressed, then went back to their tasks. A few of the men left. Carter told her they were doing fire inspections at some of the local businesses.

She tried to stay out of the way as she moved about to snap photos of the men as they worked, but when they saw her with her camera, they stopped what they were doing and hammed it up for photos, showing off their bulging muscles, lifting their T-shirts to show their hard, well-defined six-packs. Each trying to best the others.

She'd never seen so much hard, masculine flesh, and her hormones were kicking her butt and insisting she consider doing something about it. Especially since every time she turned around, either Carter or Simon would be there watching her and smiling. As if knowing that soon enough, her need would become a primal, aching desperation and they would be there for her, ready and willing to fulfill that need.

She walked into the kitchen and Kyle was cooking something in a big pot.

"Smells good," Rikki said as she breathed in the aroma, her stomach rumbling.

He grinned. "Well, the guys say my soup doesn't suck."

"Can I help?" she asked.

"No, thanks. It's done. I'll just carry the pot out to the table and then it's a free-for-all."

"What about setting the table?"

"Got it," one of the other men—Daniel, she thought his name was—said as he grabbed a stack of bowls, followed by another man carrying spoons and a stack of glasses through the door to the table.

As if my magic, all the men began arriving at the table and sitting down.

Tanner pulled out a chair for her. "Sit beside me, darlin'."

She thanked him as she sat down, then he pushed her chair into place. As he pulled out his own chair, though, Carter stepped in and sat in it.

"Thanks, buddy," Carter said with a grin.

Before Tanner could claim the seat on the other side of her, Simon had already taken his place there.

"So that's how it is," Tanner said as he moved to the next chair and sat down.

The men laughed and told stories over lunch. Mostly funny tales about missteps many of them had made, jokes they'd played on each other, or the odd people they encountered. Like the previous week when Kyle had gone barreling into a burning kitchen in a house fire to save an older woman. She didn't want to leave, so he threw her over his shoulder, but she grabbed a rolling pin from the counter and kept hitting him with it the whole time he carried her out to the ambulance.

"You guys laugh, but I've still got bruises," Kyle grumbled.

As the chuckles rumbled around the table, Simon leaned in and said, "What they didn't tell you was that Kyle discovered all the woman wanted was to save a small, clay sculpture that her granddaughter had made her. He made a point of finding the treasure on a shelf in the smoke-filled kitchen on his next trip in and returned it to her. Afterward, she baked him a huge batch of cookies in thanks."

After lunch, Rikki helped clean up the dishes, then went to where she'd left her camera in the living area. Simon and Carter were waiting for her.

"Have you decided where you're going to do the first photo shoot?" Simon asked.

"I was thinking outside. Maybe with the truck in the background."

Carter smiled. "Good thing we washed it then."

"Why don't we go out there now so you can show us where you want the truck and whatever else we can do to help you get set up?" Simon suggested.

She nodded and led the way. Once outside, she walked to the truck, which was gleaming in the sunlight, and stroked her hand along the side of it. She checked the angle of the sun and glanced around at the available space, then suggested how the vehicle could best be positioned.

"I'll move it now," Carter said.

"No, that's okay," she said. "I think we can wait until the next shift starts. I'd still like to take some more shots around the firehouse." Her excuse sounded lame, even to her.

Simon looked thoughtful as he leaned against the truck. "Rikki, are you trying to avoid taking these photos?"

Her stomach tensed. "Uh . . . why would you think that?"

"Well," he said, "it seems you've taken tons of photos of each of us in every conceivable location. I'm wondering if you're a bit nervous about having us strip down in front of you, even if only to the waist. I mean, I know you saw us do it out here this morning, but this'll be more one-on-one."

Oh, God, was she so easy to read?

Simon moved a little closer. "Is it specifically Carter and me?"

She shook her head.

"Are you uncomfortable that the others might be watching?" Carter asked.

She nodded. "A little."

"So clearing the area and leaving you with just one man—"

"Will make it worse," she said, interrupting Simon.

She gazed up at him. She didn't know how to explain her discomfort without admitting that she was completely inexperienced with men, and that this whole shoot had made her feel like she was in way over her head.

Simon's gaze locked on her, filled with concern. "You know that no one here would hurt you, right? Or make a move on you if you made it clear you didn't want him to."

She nodded, feeling a little silly admitting her nervousness to them.

"And if you're uncomfortable with the kind of teasing we all did this afternoon," Carter said, "we'll let everyone know to lay off."

She smiled. They were both so sweet to look out for her like this.

"No. It's okay. I'm just not used to doing something like this . . . I normally do weddings and prom pictures and maternity shoots. This is just . . . different for me. I'm not used to directing big authoritative men in uniforms."

Simon smiled. "We won't exactly be in uniform."

She stared up at him solemnly, very aware of his solid chest. His broad shoulders.

His masculine aura.

"Taking the clothes off doesn't change anything," she said, almost breathlessly. "The air of authority is a part of you."

And right now, it was heating her blood and making her want things she shouldn't want. To be in his arms, pulled tight against his hard chest. To feel Carter move in close behind her, sandwiching her between the heat of their large bodies.

Oh, God, without meaning to she tilted her head up, her lips aching for the feel of Simon's. Her eyes probably sending a glittering invitation to him. Simon's eyes flared to life and he seemed to lean closer. Her lips tingled, waiting for the feel of his and her breath held—

The pulsing sound of an alarm startled her.

"Ah fuck." Simon grasped her arm and planted a quick kiss on her lips, then turned and ran toward the firehouse, Carter right behind him.

Suddenly, men flooded from the doors, pulling on their jackets as they raced to the truck. She hurried out of the way as they leaped onto the vehicle, her heart thumping loudly.

Rikki paced around the firehouse, her chest tight, the old fear pulsing though her. Finally, she picked up her cell and called Cassie.

"Hey, how you doing? How are those sexy firemen treating you?"

"They're great. They're all really nice."

"What's wrong, Rikki?" Cassie asked with concern.

Rikki didn't ask Cassie how she knew. Rikki could tell that her voice was tight with tension.

"They got called out to a fire."

"They're firefighters."

"I know," Rikki snapped, then drew in a deep breath. "I'm sorry, I . . ." Her hand covered her mouth, as if that would hold back the panic, or the sobs that threatened. "I just . . . can't stop thinking about that night . . . with Jesse."

"I'll be right over."

Rikki sank onto the couch. "I don't want to take you away from work," she said halfheartedly.

"Don't worry about it. We can do some planning on how to promote the calendar. Then I *will* be working."

Fifteen minutes after hanging up, Cassie walked into the room. She sat down and slid her arm around Rikki.

"You know they'll be fine, right?" Cassie said. "They get these calls every day. Several times a day."

Rikki shook her head. "Jesse wasn't fine. He went out

that day, just like he did every other day, but that day . . ."
She blinked back tears. "*That* day, he didn't come back."

Cassie's hand slid on top of Rikki's and closed around it.

"They'll come back. All of them."

They had to come back. Rikki couldn't stand the
thought of Simon or Carter being hurt or . . . Her chest
tightened.

She didn't want any of them to get hurt.

"Did I ever tell you I was at the firehouse that day . . .
when they got the call?"

"No, you didn't," Cassie said softly.

Rikki shook her head, swiping her hand over her cheeks
and pushing her hair behind her ears, so it wouldn't be so
obvious she was wiping her eyes.

"Yeah. I dropped by to bring him some home-baked
cookies and just to see him, you know? Then the call
came in."

Cassie squeezed her hand. But Rikki felt a numbness
take over. She felt herself start to tremble.

"Just before he left, he gave me a quick kiss." Rikki's
gaze landed on Cassie's. "And then . . . he was gone."

This time she couldn't stop the tears that started to
trickle down her face, but she dashed them away as quickly
as she could.

When Simon had given her that kiss before they left, it
had brought it all back. The alarm sounding. The sense of
urgency as the men rushed toward the truck.

The pain.

And now, even thinking about the kiss with Simon—
and the fact that seconds before he'd been about to kiss her

much more passionately, probably even joined by Carter—filled her with guilt. She'd loved Jesse, yet now she was yearning to let these new men—*two* of them no less—kiss her. Touch her.

To make love to her.

"Aw, sweetie . . ." Cassie enveloped her in her arms and Rikki rested her head on her friend's shoulder as Cassie squeezed her.

After a moment of comfort in Cassie's embrace, Rikki drew back.

"You know, you never talk about Jesse," Cassie said. "I wonder if it might help. Not focusing on your loss, but on the good memories. Like how you met. Why don't you tell me about that?"

Rikki leaned back. "I guess. It happened when I was in a car accident. It was a Saturday night and my dad had loaned me the car to drive to a party. I was on my way home, driving along a quiet side street when I was broadsided. The other driver took off and I was left there all alone."

"Were you hurt?" Cassie asked.

"Not badly. Just cuts and scrapes, but at the time I was terrified. I could smell gas and all I wanted to do was get out of the car and put some distance between me and the vehicle, but the door wouldn't open. I was trapped. I tried to call 911, but my cell was out of power."

Rikki glanced at Cassie.

"That's when Jesse showed up. He'd been out for a run and he'd heard the crash. He raced up to the car and told me to stay calm. As soon as he arrived I felt better. Safer, you know?"

She hugged her knees to her chest.

"He asked if I was okay, then tried the door, but he couldn't get it open either. He called in the accident, then stayed with me the whole time. He told me he was a firefighter and that helped calm me down. I knew I was in good hands."

That and the fact that, even though she was terrified being trapped in the car, the moment she'd seen him, she'd felt that *knowing*. That he was someone very special.

"After the accident, he checked up on me several times." She smiled. "I knew it was more than professional courtesy. When we started dating, my dad wasn't too happy about it."

"Why is that?" Cassie asked.

Rikki shrugged. "He was older than me. I was barely seventeen and he was twenty-four."

Cassie laughed. "I can see how your dad wouldn't be impressed."

"But Mom was on my side. She understood that Jesse and I were meant to be together."

She'd told Mom right off about the feeling she'd had when she met him. Mom had been ecstatic. She would have preferred him to be closer to Rikki's age, but Mom didn't argue with fate.

Rikki's chest constricted. But fate had been cruel and had torn them apart in the end. Rikki could feel the tears well in her eyes again and could barely blink them back.

Cassie gave her a quick squeeze. "Okay, honey, what we need to do is get your mind off it."

Rikki smiled and nodded, wiping her damp eyes. "You're right."

Cassie smiled, too. "So how did you like washing the truck this morning with all those hot guys?"

"How did you know about that?"

"Carter told me their plan last night. I suggested the tight bathing suits." She winked. "To benefit the calendar and our charities of course."

Rikki grinned. "I'm not sure, but I think I should be mad at you."

"For what? You should count yourself lucky. I wish I got to see their packages displayed in those tiny little bathing suits."

"Okay, we're changing the subject."

Cassie laughed. "Seriously though, how did the photo shoots go?"

Rikki sighed and explained to her friend how she'd frozen up, finding herself intimidated at the thought of directing such authoritative men, even sans uniforms.

Actually, especially without their uniforms.

It was one thing to know that the uniform was intimidating, but she knew that the men themselves, their very personalities, were strong and confident. Commanding.

She didn't know how to deal with it.

"Well, then," Cassie said, patting Rikki's hand, "I'll stay and help you get started. As soon as they all come back, we'll set up outside and start taking sexy pictures of half-naked men." She grinned. "I'm willing to make the sacrifice for you."

*   *   *

It was midafternoon when the men returned. Rikki sighed in relief as they all came into the firehouse unscathed.

"See, I told you," Cassie whispered to her.

Rikki squeezed her hand. "Thanks for staying with me," she murmured back.

She glanced up to see Simon watching her as he and Carter walked in the door, sweaty, with streaks of dirt on his face. She knew by the look of concern in his eyes that he could tell she'd been worried.

"Hey, Cassie," Carter said with a smile as the two men walked toward her and Cassie. "Nice to see you. Keeping Rikki company while we were gone?"

Cassie grinned. "Any excuse to come over and see you boys. So you been out playing pool?"

"I wish," Carter responded. "It was a restaurant kitchen fire. A lot of damage, but no one was seriously hurt."

Rikki flinched at the thought that someone *was* hurt. Was it one of the firefighters? She didn't know them all yet and wasn't sure everyone who had left had also come back.

"Who was hurt?" she asked.

"The chef tried to put out the fire himself after he ensured his staff got out safely," Carter explained, "but it didn't go so well for him. He got some burns, but he'll be okay."

She felt Simon watching her and turned her gaze to him.

"You don't have to worry about us, you know," Simon said. "We do this every day."

"I wasn't worried," Rikki said in casual tone.

She stiffened under his penetrating gaze. Then he chuckled.

"I don't believe that, but at least it tells me one interesting thing."

"And what's that?" she asked tightly.

"That you care about us."

Carter smiled. "I think that means we've got a shot with you."

Her lips turned up in a thin smile. "Maybe like the proverbial snowball."

As soon as Simon and Carter left to go up the stairs to shower and change, Cassie turned to her.

"Are you nuts? They're gorgeous! Yeah, I know they're firemen and you'll worry all the time, but life is full of danger and you can't let it hold you back. People get killed in car accidents every day, but your life wouldn't be nearly as exciting if you refused to drive anywhere."

Rikki loved Cassie, but she could be annoyingly persistent. Rikki had heard this speech before.

"Okay, I'm walking away now," Rikki said.

"Oh, no you aren't. We're going to get started on that photo shoot, remember?" Cassie's face grew serious. "And I have one more thing to say."

Chapter Seven

"What is it?" Rikki asked, curious at Cassie's change of tone.

"Look, Rikki. Not everyone finds their true love as quickly as you found Jesse. The likelihood that'll happen again is slim. You'll date a few guys—maybe a lot of guys—before you find that special someone again. So why not Simon and Carter? They're hot. Sexy. And they're really great guys. They're perfect to get your feet wet." She grinned. "And other parts of you, too."

Rikki's eyes widened. "Cassie, I can't believe you said that!"

Cassie laughed. "Yeah, you were thinking it. I've seen how you look at them."

Rikki pursed her lips. "Thanks for caring so much about me. I do appreciate it. But I have to do what feels right for me."

"Okay. So I'll keep bugging you and you keep resisting." Cassie grinned. "Sounds like a plan."

A few minutes later, the men started coming down the stairs and settling into their tasks again. Tanner gave her a wink as he went by. Simon and Carter were the last to come down.

"We're all ready for you," Carter said with a smile.

"Well, I don't know about that," Cassie said, eyeing them up and down. "You were probably more ready a few minutes ago, *before* you put on those shirts."

"No problem," Carter said as he pulled off his navy T-shirt.

At the sight of his rock-hard abs, Rikki felt her hormones shooting into overdrive. Then Simon followed suit and she was faced with two broad, sexy chests.

Cassie grinned in appreciation, then grabbed Rikki's hand and started to pull her toward the door.

"Let's go take those pictures," Cassie said as she dragged Rikki along.

"I don't know. We were going to do it in front of the truck, but we probably have enough shots of the truck, now that I think about it."

"You can just take the shots in front of the firehouse," Cassie said. "They'll look great."

Simon's and Carter's long-legged strides had them to the door before Cassie and Rikki got there and Simon grinned as he opened the door for her.

"She's not letting you off the hook."

"True that," Cassie said.

They walked out into the late afternoon sunshine. The truck was inside and the wooden garage door closed.

"I'll go grab some equipment," Simon said and disappeared back into the firehouse.

Rikki decided on the best position to pose the men based on the direction of the sun. Simon returned with an axe hefted over his shoulder and two hats. He tossed one to Carter. Once they pulled them on, goose bumps danced along Rikki's flesh.

God, they were just so *sexy*.

Rikki snapped a few shorts of Simon with the axe, then Carter.

"Let's do a few with both of them," Cassie suggested.

She knew Cassie was friends with the men, but that didn't stop Cassie's eyes from glittering with unadulterated lust.

"Okay," Rikki said. "Could the two of you move close together?"

As she watched them on the camera display, they closed the distance between them, then both flexed their biceps, as if competing to see who had the biggest bulging muscles.

Rikki felt faint.

They did some poses where they looked like they were charging into a fire, fierce expressions on their faces. Then Carter posed with the axe as if swinging it, with Simon pointing as if at some danger.

After several more poses, Cassie said to the guys, "Those are all great. But maybe you want to . . . you know . . . undo the belts and lower your zippers . . . juuust a little." She grinned. "That'll have the ladies flocking to buy this calendar."

"I don't think—" Rikki started, but at the sight of the men unbuckling their belts, she fell into a daze.

When they tugged down the zippers of their jeans—
about halfway—her mouth went dry. She stared, mesmerized, a part of her screaming for them to pull those zippers
all the way down, then to . . .

Oh, God, what's gotten into me?

She realized she'd been snapping pictures without even
thinking.

Carter hooked his fingers a little under the waistband
of his boxers and pushed down. Rikki couldn't take her eyes
off the skin—lightly smattered with curls of hair—being
revealed. He only pushed the fabric down an inch or so,
but anticipation built in her as she realized she wanted—
desperately—to see what was still hidden inside. Even just
a quick peek.

Not to be outdone, Simon flattened his hands on his
hard stomach and pushed the fingers under the black waistband of his gray boxers.

Tingles danced down Rikki's spine at the thought of
what it would feel like under there. The firm, hard abdo-
men. The prickly feel of the hair as she ran her hand downward, the curls growing denser. Her fingertips brushing
against his hard shaft.

She sucked in a breath.

Maybe she should see what it was like to live on the
wild side and have casual sex with one of these guys. Maybe
having a hot, flash-fire affair with a sexy firefighter would
help her get past her frozen state in the sex department. And
ease the ache just seeing these two men elicited.

She lowered the camera and her gaze locked with
Simon's. His attention flared to life and she was sure he

could read her thoughts. She shifted her focus to Carter and a big smile claimed his lips.

Her pulse accelerated and she could feel the magnetic pull of desire drawing her closer to them. If she walked over there right now—

The blaring of the alarm made her jump, and sent her heart rate skyrocketing. She sucked in a breath as Simon and Carter grabbed their shirts and ran toward the firehouse. Cassie took hold of Rikki's hand and tugged her to the picnic table on the lawn at the side of the firehouse. They both watched as the door opened and the truck pulled out, then raced away.

Rikki shivered. Would she get used to this? If she had an affair with Simon or Carter, would every emergency tear at her insides?

Inside the firehouse, Rikki saw that someone had been preparing dinner for everyone, but it had been left on the stove. Everything was turned off, but the chicken in the pan was only half cooked. She turned on the element and started cooking it.

Cassie helped her prepare the dinner, including fresh rolls. Cassie made a salad, ready to be tossed with dressing, then covered it and put it into the fridge. When Rikki finished cooking the chicken and vegetables, she put it in a casserole dish and put that in the fridge, too, ready for their return.

"Why don't you come on back to my house?" Cassie said, once they'd cleaned up the dishes. "We can hang out. Maybe play some cards."

"No, I think I'll stay here. I want to go over the pictures I took today. See what we have. Maybe do some editing."

"You want to be here when they get back to make sure they're all okay. You can't hang out here every time they're on a call, you know."

"I know, but I can this time."

"They could be gone for hours."

Rikki shrugged. "That's okay. I took lots of pictures."

"Okay, I see I'm not going to convince you to leave. Do you want me to stay?"

Rikki rested her hand on Cassie's arm. "No, it's okay. I really do want to go through those pictures. And before you offer, I'd rather you see them after I've gone through them. Putting my best foot forward and all that."

"Okay, well if you change your mind, or you want me to come and give you a ride home later, just call."

"Will do."

She watched as Cassie left, then went and sat on the couch in the living area and opened her laptop. As she reviewed the pictures, taken in spots all over the firehouse, with faces of men she had only met today—except for Carter and Simon—she felt her heart ache at the thought of any of them getting hurt.

She opened a picture of Carter with his shirt off, one of the ones she'd taken just before they got called away. Then one of Simon. She placed them side by side on the screen and just stared at them.

She didn't know these men very well, but they were already finding a place in her heart.

She flicked through a few more images, then browsed

the ones she'd taken of the two of them. Her breath caught at how incredibly sexy they were. Broad, sculpted chests and well defined abs. When she got to the ones where they'd started teasing her by sliding their fingers under the waist-bands of their boxers, she found herself getting turned on. She couldn't help imagining pressing her hand flat on one of those hard stomachs and sliding under the fabric of his boxers, then wrapping her fingers around the stiff, thick prize inside.

Her eyes flickered closed. *Oh, God, I need to get past whatever's stopping me and just have sex with one of these men. Maybe even both of them.*

She remembered their comment about sharing things and wondered if they shared women, too. The thought of them both driving into her at the same time filled her with lust.

What was happening to her?

Ever since meeting Simon and Carter, all she could think about was sex. And now those thoughts had turned into full-on kink.

And yet she couldn't help herself. Her head might be disconnected from what her body wanted most of the time, but with Carter and Simon, the urges were clear and strong.

And that sense that she was meant to be with them . . . that was with her all the time. Anytime she saw them. Any-time she was close to them. And when they touched her, everything went haywire inside her.

It was so confusing. If her mother was right, and Rikki did have the strong intuition that so many of the women in her family had, then what did it mean? How could she possibly be meant to be with both of them?

Cassie might be right that since it didn't make sense to have that feeling for two men that it was probably her body's only way to push her into the sexual arena.

She knew it couldn't be real. Not like what she'd felt for Jesse. Because he'd been the love of her life.

She'd lost Jesse. And now she had these feelings for Simon and Carter.

She stared at their photos, the sexual stirring spiraling through her, blending with a growing sense of fear. Even though she had only known them a couple of days, somehow they'd found a place deep in her heart and she knew that if something happened to either one of them, she would be devastated.

She snapped her laptop closed and stood up, then began to pace. It was getting dark outside and she was getting tired. She didn't know how long they'd be, so she decided to take a nap. Or try to. She glanced around the room and her gaze fell to the couch and the throw blanket carefully draped over the back of it. It would be cozy on the couch, but she'd be too alert to really fall asleep in an open space like this.

She paced some more and before she knew it, she'd walked up the stairs to the second floor and down the hall to the stairway leading to Simon and Carter's room. They'd let her change in there and she was sure they wouldn't mind her taking a nap in one of their beds.

Once in the room, she opened the dresser drawer and pulled out one of the men's T-shirts. She was sure they wouldn't mind. She didn't want to sleep in her dress pants and blouse, and it would be a relief getting this bra off.

She stripped down to her panties and tugged on the big shirt. She smiled, liking the fact that this shirt that was hugging her body had been worn by one of the big men. Had caressed his skin as he'd pulled it over his head and down his chest.

She wrapped her arms around herself, glad she didn't know which man the shirt belonged to. This way, she could imagine it belonged to both of them. She could imagine she could smell their masculine scent on it.

She pulled back the covers and slid into one of the beds. As she pulled the sheet around herself, she could imagine one of the men wrapping his arms around her and holding her close. With that comforting feeling, she soon found herself drifting off.

Rikki opened her eyes to darkness.

She glanced at the clock on the bedside table. It was after ten.

She sat upright. Where were Carter and Simon and the others? Had they still not returned?

Her heart clenched as she pushed the sheets back and got up. She opened the bedroom door and peered into the hallway.

The light was on. Maybe they were back. But it was so quiet.

She couldn't remember if it had been on when she'd come up here. She hadn't turned on the bedroom light because the light from the setting sun had been streaming in the windows, but the hall would have been dark. She might have turned it on when she came up the stairs.

She rubbed her eyes, wondering if she should go downstairs and wait for them. It would be nicer for them to come back to a cheery, well-lit living room than the gloomy darkness.

As she turned, she thought she heard voices. She cocked her head. Yes, that was Simon's voice. Coming from her right.

She stepped out of the bedroom and hurried to the last door at the end of the hall. She pushed it open and rushed in. There were some lockers along one side and some wooden benches. On the other side were white tiled walls and . . . open showers.

She halted and her eyes widened. Sure enough, there were Simon and Carter. They were facing the tiled wall, water pouring over them and . . .

Oh, God, they were totally naked.

Chapter Eight

Rikki couldn't drag her gaze away.

Muscular thighs. Bulging biceps. Tight, firm butts.

A hot fever blazed through her as she stared at them, mesmerized. Her body aching. A need pulsing through her that was so deep and compelling it felt like it would consume her.

Simon turned around.

Her eyes widened and she averted her gaze. But not before she got an eyeful of his long, thick cock.

"Rikki, what are you doing here?" he asked.

"Rikki?" Carter turned around, too.

She tried not to look. She really did. But her gaze shot to Carter's large member. Not as long as Simon's, but thicker.

Oh, God, and both their cocks were swelling.

"I'm sorry, I didn't mean to . . . I heard your voices, so I just rushed in."

"But why are you even here in the firehouse?" Carter asked.

"I wanted to go over the photos before I left and . . ."

She bit her lip. "Well, I wanted to be here when you got back. I was worried."

Simon's face beamed with a smile. "Like I said. You care about us." He held out his hand. "Now come and join us."

Shock vaulted through her. "What? Oh, no. I couldn't."

"You clearly want to or you'd be gone by now," he said as he strolled her way, the pleasant smile on his face totally non-threatening.

But she was intensely aware of his potent masculine aura. And his total nudity.

He moved behind her and wrapped his big fingers around her upper arms. His touch sent rippling waves pulsing through her body. He guided her toward the shower.

"Let's get this T-shirt off you," he said as he grasped the hem of the loose-fitting garment and started to pull it up.

She sucked in a breath and pushed it back down. "No, I can't . . ."

Simon turned her to face him and stroked some loose strands of hair from her face, sending tingles dancing through her.

"Rikki, I think you want to do this."

"I think she's just a little shy," Carter said, now standing by her side. "Maybe this will help." He took her hand and tugged her under the water.

She sucked in a breath as the warm spray soaked the white T-shirt. The men's gazes fell to her chest and their eyes darkened. She glanced down and realized she might as well be naked because every detail of her breasts clearly showed through the drenched fabric.

Simon's hand glided around her body and over her

breasts, cupping them in his big hands. When his thumbs glided over her nipples—which were now as hard as beads—she nearly jumped at the intense sensations. She leaned back against him, welcoming the support of his body.

Carter moved closer and ran one hand up her stomach, then pushed under one of Simon's hands and cupped her. Simon shifted his hand to her shoulder, then drew her long hair back and his lips nuzzled her neck, sending delightful tingles dancing down her spine.

Carter squeezed her breast lightly, then leaned forward and took her cloth-covered nipple in his mouth and suckled.

"Oh, God," she whimpered.

Her head fell back against Simon's shoulder as Carter pulled on the hem of her shirt and peeled it upward.

She should stop this, but she couldn't find the strength. Her breath caught in her lungs as he pulled it above her breasts. The smile that spread across his face, paired with the look of absolute awe, held her transfixed.

Carter pulled her shirt the rest of the way off. Now she stood between them wearing only her small, white lace panties.

She could feel something hard and thick against her back and . . . Oh, God, she knew it was Simon's cock swelling into an erection. Her gaze fell to Carter's cock and it was standing upright like a flagpole.

She shivered as she tried to tug her gaze away from it. It was so much bigger than it had been when she'd first seen it dangling free a few minutes ago.

Seeing where she was looking, Carter smiled and wrapped his hand around it and moved closer. He reached for her hand and drew it to his erection, then guided her to wrap her fingers around him. The feel of his thick member in her hand . . . of it pulsing within her grip . . . made her heart beat faster.

She stood frozen, part of her insisting she pull her hand away, but the excitement that shimmered through her at the feel of his thick, hard flesh in her grip—so powerful and thrilling—made her feel ultra-feminine. And needy.

Simon's hand enveloped one of her breasts again as he swept her long, wet hair over her shoulder. His lips nuzzled along her collarbone, triggering a wave of tremors inside her. Carter stepped closer still and cupped her face, then tipped it up and, with a warm glow in his eyes, dipped down and captured her lips.

It was heaven feeling Carter's mouth moving on hers. She found herself responding to his kiss with breathless enthusiasm. His arm curled around her waist and he drew her close to his body, pressing his cock, with her hand still tightly around it, between their bodies. Her other arm slid up his broad, naked chest to his shoulder, then curled around his neck.

Carter deepened the kiss, as Simon continued to kiss her neck and shoulder. Simon's hips rocked, gliding his solid cock up and down her lower back. Carter slid a hand down her stomach and—

"Ohhh."

The feel of his fingers dipping into her panties, then

gliding over her slickness, sent a vibrant, needy heat through her. But when they curled and started to slip into her passage, she grabbed his wrist and pushed it away.

Carter's gaze locked with hers. "What is it, Rikki?"

"I . . ." She bit her lip. "I'm not ready."

A smile spread across his face. "From what I felt, you're more than ready."

Her cheeks flushed hotly.

"I . . ." She shook her head, pressing one hand against Carter's chest to put a little distance between them. "You don't understand. I've never . . ."

Her words trailed off. She couldn't just baldly say it.

"But you find the idea exciting, right?" Simon asked. "Being with the two of us?"

She nodded. "I do, but that's not what I meant."

She realized she still had Carter's sizable cock nestled in her fingers. She drew her hand away.

"What *do* you mean, Rikki?" Carter asked.

"I . . . well, it's really that . . ." She bit her lip again. "I've never done this at all."

"This being . . . ?" Carter prompted, his amber eyes turned serious.

"I've never been with a man before. I'm a . . . virgin."

Behind her, Simon's body stiffened. "Fuck. Really?"

"But at the club that night . . . You seemed pretty eager to be with us," Carter said.

She nodded. "I was tired of being a twenty-six-year-old virgin. I was sick of being afraid. I'd moved to a new town . . . was making a new start . . . So I wanted to move forward." She dropped her gaze. "I was attracted to the two of you . . . and you were so nice . . . I thought . . . why not them?"

She shivered. She wasn't quite under the spray of water, and was cold at the loss of their warm bodies so close to hers. Simon noticed and took her hand, then guided her to the wooden benches. He grabbed a big white towel and wrapped it around her, then settled her on the bench. The men sat on either side of her.

Simon rested his hand on her shoulder. "You said you were engaged. How is it you and he never took this step?"

"I told you. I was young. He was seven years older than me and we were waiting until my eighteenth birthday." She pursed her lips. "But he died three weeks before that."

Carter slid his arm around her and drew her close. She patted her wet face with the edge of the towel around her, partly to wipe away the tears forming.

"I understand your pain, sweetheart," Simon said, "and how difficult it must have been for you. And still is. But it's been a long time." He tucked his finger under her chin and tipped it up. "You're right that it's time to move on."

His face dipped to hers and their mouths met. The gentle, coaxing pressure of his kiss . . . the light brush of his tongue against her lips . . . and the tip of his tongue tenderly sweeping inside . . . took her breath away.

Simon released her and Carter turned her face to him, then kissed her. His lips were more insistent, more demanding, but still tender and loving. She opened to his tongue as she had for Simon and it dashed inside, then glided over her own. Ripples of need sent her head spinning. And she could feel wetness pooling between her legs.

"Rikki, we'll do whatever you want. If you want us to back off, we'll do it. But we'll also help you through this."

"You make it sound like I have a disease." Which she knew was totally unfair of her to say. They were being sweet and supportive.

"Not at all," Simon said. "Losing your virginity can be a beautiful thing." He stroked her cheek and his big hand cupped her face. "But you want it to be with someone who'll be patient and gentle."

"You've already admitted you're attracted to us," Carter said.

She drew in a deep breath. They were right. She didn't want to live like this anymore. Wanting something she wouldn't give in to. Being afraid of taking that step.

She trusted them. And the strong feeling she was meant to be with them . . . it had to mean that this was the right step.

And God knew, she wanted them. Desperately.

She bit her lip, then she nodded.

She stood up and released the towel that was wrapped around her, carelessly letting it fall to the tiled floor. The heat of their glittering masculine gazes sent heat tingling over her skin.

They both stood up, their wilted cocks pushing upward again.

"So which of us do you choose?" Simon asked.

"*Both* of you," she said, then held out her hands.

God, the thought of sinking his big, hard cock into her had Carter's groin aching. Her adorable derriere swayed as she led them toward the door. He could barely wait to strip those little lacy panties off her.

"Wait," she said as she stopped short. "Where are the other men?"

"They're all asleep," Simon said. "Carter and I came up about twenty minutes later than the others because we had to do some final checks and finish up some things. By the time we got up here, they were all in bed. Where were you, anyway?"

"I fell asleep in your bedroom while I waited for you. I didn't think you'd mind."

Carter smiled. "Of course we don't mind."

She pushed the door open and peered out, then led them into the bedroom, which was only a few steps away. Once in the bedroom, she turned to them and smiled.

Simon walked across the room and closed the drapes, then sat on his bed.

"Rikki, it's great that you want to be with both of us, but only one of us can be the one to take your virginity."

"Does it matter to you which one?" she asked. "Because I really don't want to choose between you. And I still want to make love with both of you." She smiled. "Maybe you could blindfold me so I won't know which of you is actually the one. That way, anytime I'm with either of you afterward, I can imagine you were my first."

Carter's cock twitched. God, that was so hot.

Simon grinned. "I like that you're already talking about this being an ongoing thing."

"You weren't thinking of not calling me afterward,

were you?" she asked, her eyes glittering as her cute little lips turned up in a grin.

Carter wrapped his hands around her waist and nuzzled her neck. "Of course not. With the heat between us, I can't see this ending anytime soon."

"Well, not before we're done with the calendar, anyway," she murmured breathlessly.

He slid his arm around her waist and drew her to him as he stroked back her long auburn hair with the other hand. The feel of her soft, naked body against him made his cock swell even more.

Her statement made it clear she was still resisting her attraction to them. He wanted to tell her he saw this relationship between them becoming something much more serious, but one step at a time. Yesterday—hell, fifteen minutes ago—she wasn't willing to give them a chance at all.

Now she was nearly naked, pressed against his naked body, with Simon watching from the bed.

Carter's mouth danced along her neck as he coiled her long hair around his fingers. Her skin pebbled in goose bumps against his lips, setting his groin on fire. His other hand glided over her breast and he cupped it. God, her nipple was so hard it was drilling into his palm.

Simon stood up and approached, his eyes darkening. Carter released her hair as Simon stepped close behind her and turned her head, tipping up her chin. Then he found her mouth. His fingers glided through her hair as his tongue pulsed into her. Carter could feel her body quiver between them.

Simon's hand brushed Carter's as he moved it to her un-claimed breast. Carter slid downward and slid his fingers underneath her lacy panties and . . . Oh, fuck, the feel of her silky slick pussy was enough to drive any man insane with lust. He wanted to bend her over right now and plunge deep into her.

He sucked in a breath. Damn it, he wasn't the man for this. He'd never deflowered a fucking virgin before. This was too important to fuck up.

Rikki's breathing was erratic. He stroked over her soft folds, his cock pulsing in need at the feel of her velvety arousal.

She was clearly turned on. Ready. Waiting.

He glanced up, locking gazes with Simon. He was still kissing Rikki, but Carter had his attention.

"Rikki," Carter said. "I think it should be Simon."

Simon released Rikki's lips, his gaze turning to Carter.

"You didn't like my blindfold idea?" she murmured breathlessly.

"Fuck, baby," Carter said. "I love the idea of blindfolding you." He stroked her folds again, loving her small gasp. "But I think you should gaze into the eyes of the man who first takes you. You should know. And Simon's cock might be longer than mine, but it's not as thick, so it will be easier on you. Also, the guy's got way more patience and control for slow and steady than me. I'm afraid once I feel your sweet, velvety pussy around me, I won't have the discipline to go slow enough for you. Not the very first time."

Rikki drew in a deep breath. It was hard to think straight while Carter's hand was inside her panties, stroking her sensitive, slick folds.

"I wish you could both be my first."

"I have an idea," Simon said as he stroked her cheek, his deep blue eyes glimmering with heat. "How about Carter gives you your first non-solo orgasm? Before I make love to you."

Her eyes widened as Carter—chuckling—stroked her slit with his big fingers. Oh, God, she wanted someone inside her.

She instantly got her wish. One of Carter's large fingers slid into her. She stiffened as it glided into her canal, then found herself squeezing around it.

"Oh, fuck, baby," Carter murmured against her ear, his breath sending quivers along her neck.

Simon took her hand and drew her and Carter to the bed. Carter's finger slipped from inside her and he turned her around, then sat her on the edge. Simon guided her to lie back. Carter drew her panties downward. Her cheeks flushed as he exposed her intimate flesh, then tugged her panties down her thighs and to the floor. Her cheeks flushed hotter at the awareness of their frank gazes taking in the sight of her totally naked body.

She'd never been naked in front of a man before. Now she had two of them thoroughly examining every inch of her. Desire blazing in their eyes. Their cocks thrusting straight up.

Knowing how much they wanted her helped put her at ease. Carter smiled, then knelt in front of her. His hands cupped her breasts and she arched against him, her whole body quivering with excitement and need. His hands slid down to her stomach. Then lower.

Simon moved to the other side of the bed, kneeling on the floor behind her, and his hands caressed her swollen breasts, his fingers lightly stroking her hard, ultra-sensitive nubs.

Carter's hands now stroked her inner thighs. Soft, gentle strokes. She found herself opening to him. He chuckled and lifted her legs, draping them over his shoulders. Then he leaned forward and—

"Ohhhh," she moaned as his tongue laved over her wet flesh.

She arched, wanting more. He buried his mouth deeper and his tongue pushed inside her. She sucked in a breath. He drew back and smiled at her, his mouth glistening with her arousal.

He stroked her with his fingertips, then she felt him open her up and his gaze locked on her down there. When he leaned forward this time, his tongue found that very special spot. But the feel of him touching her clit like that, gently with the tip of his finger, was so much better than her own touch.

Then his tongue dragged over it and she moaned.

"I think you like what Carter's doing," Simon said against her ear, his hands still cupping her breasts.

"Yeah," she managed in a short, gaspy breath.

Her head lolled on the bed as Carter's tongue caressed her. Nuzzling and stroking. Then he suckled and pleasure swelled through her.

"Oh, Carter." She arched against him.

She felt his finger glide inside her, his mouth still working on her. Her breathing increased as her nerve endings prickled with need. He slid another finger inside her and her body automatically squeezed around him.

"Fuck, Simon, she is so tight."

Simon grinned. "I can hardly wait to be inside you, sweetheart," he said as he stroked back her hair.

But what Carter was doing to her . . . his mouth suckling her clit . . . his fingers now moving inside her in gentle thrusts . . . had her gasping for air. Pleasure coiled inside her, a spiral of need expanding through her whole being.

"Oh, Carter, please. I need . . ." She whimpered.

"What is it, baby? What do you need?" He covered her with his mouth again, but his gaze stayed locked on hers.

His eyes, so deep and brown, as warm as melting chocolate, moved her.

"I need you to . . ." She moaned again at the exquisite feel of his soft suckle. "Oh, God, please, make me come."

Simon laughed joyfully. Carter suckled her harder now, his fingers gliding in and out. She was so close. She was desperate to feel that release. But she knew the more desperate she became, the more difficult . . .

His tongue did a magic swirl then pulsed as his fingers continued to pump into her, gliding deeper than before. The pleasure—coiled so tight it ached within her—finally exploded. She moaned, her eyes widening, then falling closed as she arched against Carter's face, squeezing his fingers so tight inside her she was afraid she'd crush them.

But he kept thrusting.

She sucked in a breath, then wailed. The orgasm flashed through her, hot and intense. As it faded, she sucked in a breath, only to find it rise again as Carter continued to suckle her, his fingers still pumping deep inside her.

The bliss went on and on, until he finally took pity on her and slowed down, allowing her to gulp in some air.

He tipped her over the edge one more time before he finally let her settle back to earth.

She lay on the bed gasping, the two men smiling over her. Her eyelids fell closed for a moment, then she felt a big hand glide over her stomach. Her eyelids fluttered open.

"Are you ready for your second first?" Simon asked. He was the one kneeling in front of her now.

Chapter Nine

Rikki nodded, a little nervous, but knowing she wanted to take this step with him.

"Well, we know you're good and wet." Simon's hand glided over his hard cock as he stroked it.

She wanted to touch it. To feel its hardness. Its heat. But she didn't want to slow him down. She wanted to feel that big, thick member inside her.

Carter sat on the end of the bed, turned toward her. She wrapped her hand around his hard cock and squeezed.

"I want you inside me, Simon," she said as she began to stroke Carter. She couldn't believe how soft the skin was. And how hard the muscle beneath. It was like solid marble. She moved her hand up and down, feeling the kid leather–soft flesh glide over the rigid shaft beneath.

Simon ran his fingertips over her soaking wet flesh as he continued to stroke his long cock.

She turned to Carter, watching his cock glide within her grip.

"I want to feel yours. In my mouth."

Carter's eyes flared, and he moved closer. She turned her head and pressed her lips to his cockhead. She lapped her tongue over his tip, tasting a salty droplet. She opened wider and he pushed his cock into her mouth until the tip was inside.

"Sweetheart, I'm going to go slowly. If you want me to stop, let me know," Simon said.

She nodded, squeezing her mouth around Carter's cock. He rocked his hips, pushing it in short strokes within her mouth.

She felt something hard and hot press against her slick flesh. Simon glided his cock up and down her slit, driving her wild with need.

She wrapped her hand around Carter's cock and plucked it from her mouth, keeping a firm grip on it.

"I want it inside me," she insisted to Simon, then popped Carter's big cockhead back into her mouth.

"Patience, love. I'm going to go slow."

He pressed forward a little and her flesh stretched around him. She squeezed Carter in her mouth, nervousness rippling through her, but also intense need. When she began to suckle, Carter moaned.

Delight quivered through her at the sense of power that gave her.

Simon pushed a little deeper. She sucked in a breath.

"Does it hurt, baby?" Carter asked, stroking the hair from her face.

She slid from his cock. "A little. But"—she glanced at Simon—"please don't stop."

"I won't, love." Simon's eyes were dark with need.

He pushed deeper and the pain increased. Her eyelids fell closed, but she grabbed onto Carter's cock and pushed the tip between her lips again and sucked. Deep and hard. Focusing on the hot, hard flesh in her mouth.

Simon's long cock glided deeper into her opening, moving very slowly, but relentlessly pushing forward. Then she felt his lips on her breast and she arched. He suckled, drawing her bud deep into his mouth.

Simon continued to push into her. He lifted her legs and wrapped them around his waist, smiling as he watched her.

"I want you to come in my mouth, Carter. As Simon fucks me."

Carter chuckled. "For a virgin, you have some mouth on you." He stroked his fingertip over her lower lips.

She smiled wickedly. "Guess I'm making up for lost time."

Then he pushed his cock into her mouth again.

Simon's cock drew back, then eased forward again, starting a ripple of awareness deep inside her. Her inner flesh sensitized to the feel of the large shaft pushing inside her. Both pleasure and pain mingling together.

"I know this hurts, baby, but once you get used to it, it's going to feel incredible. Just relax—I'm going to take it very slow."

She thought of the intense orgasm Carter had given her and knew he was telling the truth.

"I'm going to push in all the way now, love." Simon gazed at her with a gentleness that tugged at her heart. Then he pushed deeper. Relentlessly. Filling her all the way.

Little flashes of light burst across the inside of her eyelids at the pain. She hadn't even realized she'd scrunched her eyelids closed. But now his body was tight against her, his long cock fully inside.

She drew in deep breaths, insisting her body relax. Carter remained still, not wanting to distract her from her concentration. But after a few moments, in the quiet interlude, her body relaxed, despite the big cock immersed inside her tight opening.

She twirled her tongue over the tip of Carter's cock and he rocked his hips forward, filling her deeper.

Simon drew back, his cock dragging along her sensitive inner canal, pleasure sparking along her nerve endings. When he glided forward again, it was easier, her increased slickness easing the way.

Carter drew his cock from her mouth, wrapping his own hand around it. When she gazed at him questioningly, he smiled.

"I want you to enjoy this." Carter's hand stroked his shaft and the sight added fuel to her rising desire.

Simon drew back, then eased forward again. The pain was almost forgotten and a new, more intense sensation took over. A beautiful, blissful delight.

She felt like he owned her body. And he knew how to make it sing. Exquisite sensations quivered through her. A yearning built inside her. Stronger and deeper with each stroke of Simon's cock. Her heart pounded and she got lost in the melting heat of his eyes.

As if reading her need, he leaned in and kissed her.

"I'm going to make you come, sweetheart. Just like Carter did. You want that, don't you?"

She nodded. "Yes," she whispered against his mouth.

His cock stretched her as it glided in and out of her, but now it felt so good. She covered her breasts and stroked them. Heat flared in the men's eyes as they watched her squeeze her soft mounds.

Simon sped up and blissful sensations fluttered through every part of her, but centered in her core. That sensitive canal where Simon filled her again and again with his pulsing cock.

"Oh, God, that feels so good." Her reedy voice quivered and she drew in a breath.

She was getting close. Ecstasy just a heartbeat away.

Her hand flung out and wrapped around Carter's cock and pulled it to her mouth. She wrapped her lips around it, then sucked on his cockhead.

Simon kept thrusting into her. Deep, fast strokes now. She gazed up at Carter, her eyes pleading. He nodded and rocked his hips, gliding his cock in short strokes inside her mouth. As she sucked on him, she closed her eyes and allowed the sensations sparking through her belly to take hold.

Then it began. The edges of her reality swirling like the waves of the ocean tide licking over on the sand. Pulsing and building. Then sizzling into a steamy surge of bliss.

She moaned around the big, hard flesh in her mouth, still pulsing in and out. Then Carter groaned and thrust deeper. A hot fountain shot into her throat and she squeezed him tighter between her lips, her body quaking in the midst of her own orgasm.

Carter slipped from her mouth and she moaned. Simon's

gaze as he thrust into her again and again was fierce. He thrust deeper and then pulled her tight, groaning.

She felt an eruption inside her. Heat pulsing into her as he came.

As she plunged over the edge one more time, she felt a deep sense of fulfillment at the fact she had satisfied both of these sexy, experienced men. As she lay on the bed panting, she hadn't realized that part of her had feared disappointing any man she was with. Because of her inexperience.

She smiled.

Simon's cock slipped from her body and he scooped her into his arms and settled her into the bed, then snuggled up behind her. She gazed up at Carter. He smiled and headed to the other bed, but she didn't want him so far away. He must have been able to read it in her eyes, so he pushed the other bed against this one and lay down in front of her. She wrapped her arm around his waist and snuggled against his shoulder.

Just before she fell asleep, she decided that following those intuitive feelings of hers was definitely a good idea.

Rikki started awake at the sound of the emergency alarm. Her eyelids opened as the big, warm body holding her close from behind slid away. Lips brushed her neck.

Carter, who was in front of her, sat up, pushing his hair from his face.

"Just go back to sleep," Carter said, then leaned in and kissed her.

She sat up and watched as both men pulled on their

clothes in record time and hurried from the room. She lay back in the bed, turmoil coiling through her as she stared into the darkness.

She'd done it. She'd given herself to two firefighters. She'd given her *virginity* to them. It didn't matter which one technically was the first. They were both a part of it.

They were both caring, wonderful men and Rikki knew this was more than just a fling. She hadn't known Simon and Carter very long, but she knew them well enough to know that she was falling for them.

And that was crazy because she knew that she could lose one or both of them in the blink of an eye.

She wrapped her arms around herself and closed her eyes, but sleep didn't come.

Rikki paid the Uber driver and went into the house. It was just after two in the morning and the place was quiet. She was tired, but the idea of going and lying in bed again, staring into the darkness, letting her thoughts wander, wasn't appealing.

She filled the kettle and turned it on, then perused the collection of teas Anna had told her to feel free to try. She grabbed an herbal one that the package claimed was a good nighttime choice with a "heavenly floral aroma." She tossed a bag in a mug, then waited for the water to boil.

When she sat down, the steaming mug in her hand, she breathed in the fragrant tea and smiled. It was a nice calming scent. Just what she needed. She sipped the hot tea and sat back in the chair, staring around the small kitchen.

She missed her place in Ashton. It hadn't been a big place, but it had been her own. With her own personal touches. Not that she didn't like living with her roommates, and it was a big help not to shoulder the whole rent.

And she liked living in the same town as Cassie. They'd been best friends in college, but after graduation Cassie had returned to Muldone and Rikki had moved back home to Ashton. Despite the distance, though, they'd kept in touch, and Rikki had always wished they could live in the same town. When a sweep of layoffs at the department store chain where Rikki worked left her without a job, she'd felt it was the perfect time to pick up and move to Muldone.

She sighed. She knew it was just that she was mourning her old life. Missing the familiar and the sense of knowing who she was. Now she was in a new town, trying to find work, making new friends.

And having sex with men.

Her stomach tightened.

Being with Simon and Carter had been exciting and . . . oh, God, so intensely pleasurable . . . but how could she have let herself get involved with them? With their job, they could get hurt . . . or die . . . at any time. Some women could deal with that. Having a partner who put his life on the line every single day. Could understand their bravery and need to save people, even at the expense of their own safety. She wished she could be like that. Had once thought she was.

But the pain of losing Jesse . . . that intense, devastating loss . . . was too much for her to bear again.

She sipped her tea. She should run. Far and fast.

But the memory of their big bodies next to her. Their large hands stroking . . . caressing . . . giving her so much delightful pleasure.

She remembered Carter's tongue gliding over her . . . the swell of pleasure inside her. Never had she experienced anything like that before.

Then when Simon had entered her . . . his big cock sliding inside her . . . being the first man to ever breach her body . . . She'd felt so vulnerable, but at the same time, so protected. The two of them had made her first time a wonderful experience. A perfect memory.

The door opened and Tina and Anna walked into the kitchen.

"Hey, there," Tina said. "You just get in?"

"Yeah," Rikki said.

Anna dropped her large, cloth shoulder bag onto the counter and pushed her straight brown hair behind her ear as she glanced at Rikki's cup.

"Good, you're trying the tea," Anna said, noting the discarded tea bag on a saucer on the counter.

"The kettle's still hot if you want one," Rikki said.

"No, thanks," Anna said. "I'm heading to bed in a minute. I want to let you know that I talked to my boss and she said that there might be a position opening up in the candle shop in a couple of weeks if you want to apply."

"Thanks, Anna. I appreciate that."

It would be fun working at the little shop with Anna, not only because of the whimsical and fragrant soaps they sold, but because of the beautiful tourist area where it was located, along the lakeshore.

Tina sat in the chair across from Rikki as Anna walked to the stairs.

She grinned. "Were you out with those sexy firefighters tonight?"

"I was at the firehouse all day and I was doing some work after they went out on a call this evening and fell asleep."

"Oh, yeah, and did one of them find you in his bed like Goldilocks? And did he make everything *just right*?"

Rikki shot her a playful glare.

"Actually, your story is more like the big bad wolf—and I mean *bad* in the very best sense of the word."

The bright smile on Tina's face made Rikki laugh.

Tina leaned forward and pushed some of Rikki's hair behind her ear as she stared into Rikki's eyes intently.

"You see, your face has that unmistakable glow that tells me something happened with those guys." She shook her head. "But in your eyes I see anxiety."

Tina leaned back and Rikki released the breath she didn't even realize she'd been holding.

"So I think you took a risk that scared you tonight, but sweetie, I just want to urge you to push through that fear. Because what you'll find on the other side will be so rewarding."

Rikki sucked in a breath. "How do you know?"

Tina smiled. "Because no matter what happens, you will have grown."

Rikki finally fell into her own bed, her body insisting on more sleep, Tina's words still echoing in her brain.

Tina was right. She shouldn't run away from this. She'd finally taken the huge step of giving her virginity to a man. She had trusted both Simon and Carter with her first time, and they had been worthy of that trust. To walk away now wouldn't be fair to them. Or to her.

She just needed to ensure she kept this relationship as a casual fling. Which is the only thing that made sense anyway, since she was involved with two of them. It's not like she'd wind up getting married and having kids with both of them. And choosing one of them over the other at this point could damage their friendship.

So as long as she didn't fall in love with either one of them, there should be no problem.

But having sex with them . . . her eyelids fell closed . . . that was worth her diligence. To feel the heat of their touch . . . their tenderness . . .

She yawned and rolled onto her side. Her body drifted. The alarm went off.

Her eyelids popped open. It was full daylight outside.

She sat up and pushed the covers aside, then blinked at the sunlight streaming in the window. Birds chirped in the trees in the backyard and she smiled.

She'd had sex last night. Her smile broadened, feeling like it would crack her face, but she didn't care. And it had been heaven on earth!

She leaped up and headed to the shower. Once she was dressed, she raced downstairs and headed into the kitchen to put some coffee on, only to find Mel had beat her to it.

"Morning," he said. "You want some coffee, too?"

"Yes, thanks." But Rikki noticed he already had enough water for several cups.

A woman walked into the kitchen, wearing a sexy green dress that hugged her curves. She had a big smile on her face.

"Morning," the tall brunette said, gazing at Mel with a glowing smile.

He smiled back as she slid into his arms for a kiss. "Hello there."

Mel wore only his jeans and the woman's hands glided over his bare chest. Rikki wasn't sure if she should drift into the living room, leaving them with their privacy or not.

The kiss ended and Mel smiled at her. "Tammy, this is one of my roommates, Rikki."

"Hi, Rikki." Tammy stuck her hand out and Rikki shook it.

"Go sit down and I'll make breakfast," Mel said to Tammy, then watched her swaying backside as she walked to the table.

Rikki couldn't help laughing at his sheepish grin.

A knock sounded at the front door and Tammy got up. "I'll get it."

"Want to join us for breakfast?" Mel grabbed the eggs from the fridge. "I'm cooking."

"That would be great, thanks."

"Oh, Rikki," Tammy said as she walked into the kitchen again. "There's someone here to see you."

Right behind her were Simon and Carter.

Chapter Ten

"Good morning," Rikki said, her heart swelling at the sight of them.

But their expressions were serious.

"Good morning," Simon said.

"This is my roommate, Mel," she said, gesturing to Mel, "and his friend, Tammy."

"Happy to meet you," Tammy said, her gaze taking in their handsome faces and broad, muscular frames. "Are you Rikki's brothers?"

"No, we're working on a project together, and we're . . . friends."

"What kind of project?" Tammy asked.

"Simon and Carter are firefighters," Rikki said, "and my friend Cassie and I are putting together a calendar to help their firehouse raise funds for a worthwhile charity."

Tammy smiled. "So you're taking sexy pictures of these guys? You lucky thing."

"Down, girl," Mel said with a smile.

Tammy curled her arm around his waist. "Don't worry. You're still number one."

But Rikki could tell from the glint in Tammy's eyes that she was okay with there being a number two. And maybe even a number three.

Mel stared at Carter. "Hey, man, didn't you go to Weston Heights High School?" Then he grinned. "You were on the football team. You won the big game senior year with that amazing touchdown."

"Yeah, well, it was a team effort," Carter said.

"Sure, but you're the one who scored the points. And didn't you used to date Emily Saunders, head cheerleader? You two seemed pretty serious. Did you make a go of it?"

Carter shook his head. "No. She headed off for college and I joined the fire department."

"Did you go to school around here, too?" Mel asked Simon.

"No, I lived in Claremont, about an hour north of here, until I graduated. This guy," he nudged his head toward Carter, "and I met in training."

"If it weren't for Simon, I might not have made it through," Carter said.

"If you played football," Rikki said, "I'm surprised you'd have trouble with the training."

Carter's amber eyes grew sad. "That was around the time I lost my parents. They died in a car accident. Simon helped me stay focused and kept pushing me through extra drills to take my mind off it."

Simon gripped Carter's shoulder and squeezed.

No one said anything for a few moments, then Mel broke the silence.

"I'm just making breakfast. Would you like to join us?"

Tammy smiled. "Please do."

"Thanks for the invitation, but we came to ask Rikki out to lunch," Simon said. "We have something we want to discuss with her." He glanced at Rikki. "What do you say?"

"Okay," Rikki said. She turned to Mel. "Thanks for offering to make me breakfast."

"Who's making who breakfast?" Tina said as she stepped into the kitchen. "'Cause I'll take that offer." Then she noticed Simon and Carter. "Oh, a full house." She smiled at the men. "Nice to see you again."

"We're just on our way out," Simon said as he grasped Rikki's hand and led her from the room.

Rikki glanced around and Tina gave her a nod, a big smile on her face.

Simon got in the driver's seat as Carter opened the passenger door for her. Once she slid inside, Carter got in the back, but leaned toward her.

"You were gone when we got back from our call," Carter said. "We wanted to make sure everything was okay."

"Of course. Why wouldn't it be?"

"Because, "Simon said, "you took a big step last night. We wanted to make sure you weren't having second thoughts." He took her hand. "That you weren't regretting what happened."

She shook her head. "No regrets. What we did last night was wonderful. I want to thank you for making it a perfect first time for me."

"But?" Carter asked.

She turned to him and smiled. "No buts. And to prove it, instead of going out to lunch, why don't we just go back to your place? Then we can do what we were going to do that first night you took me home."

Carter laughed heartily. "You don't need to ask me twice."

Simon started the car and pulled forward. Soon they were zooming to what Rikki was sure would be the next most exciting experience of her life.

Rikki followed Simon and Carter into their house, but as she started toward the stairs, Simon caught her hand.

"You haven't eaten yet. We meant it when we said we want to feed you."

She laughed. "You're really going to pick food over sex?"

His mouth curled up in a smile. "We're not choosing one over the other. We have all day."

Carter took her other hand and kissed it. "And we want you to keep your strength up."

They tugged her into the kitchen.

"Just sit down and we'll make you something," Simon said.

Carter started to lead her to the table by the window, but she slipped her hand free.

"At least let me make lunch." She peered around Simon into the fridge he'd opened.

"I was going to throw some burgers onto the barbeque," Simon said.

"Okay, well, you two men can manage the fire-burning apparatus," she said, "while I make a salad."

Carter chuckled. "Technically, it's a gas-burning apparatus."

She raised an eyebrow. "It involves fire and gas so that's your department."

The men took some hamburger patties from the fridge and Carter put spices on them, then brushed on some barbeque sauce while she started slicing vegetables for the salad. Once she finished the salad and tossed in the dressing, she walked to the patio doors and went outside.

"How are the burgers?" she asked.

"Almost done," Carter said as he flipped one.

"It's a beautiful day," Simon said. "Why don't we eat out here?"

The barbeque was on a large wooden deck and beyond the steps was a patio leading to a kidney-shaped pool glittering in the sunlight. There was even a hot tub sunken into the deck.

"Sounds like a great idea," she said. "This is a beautiful backyard."

"Thanks. This was my parents' place. I inherited it a few years ago. Dad installed pools for a living and he put this in when I was a kid. We spent a lot of happy hours in this backyard."

At his wistful expression she could tell he missed his dad.

She followed Simon back into the house and together they brought out buns, condiments, and the salad. The men had already brought out a pile of plates and Carter placed a plate of neatly stacked burgers on the center of the picnic table on the deck.

Rikki sat down facing the pool.

"You have a nice little slice of heaven here," she said.

"You like the water?" Carter asked.

"I love it." She grabbed a bun from the basket and placed a patty inside. "So have you two lived together long?"

"Yeah, for a few years now," Carter said. "We've been friends for a long time, and it's much easier living with someone who's on the same type of shift."

"And who understands the demands of the job," Simon said.

She bit into the burger. It was delicious. Simon poured her some lemonade, the ice tinkling against the jug.

"So why did you decide to become firefighters?" she asked.

Carter shrugged. "It's all I've ever wanted to be. My uncle was a firefighter and he'd take me to the house sometimes. They'd let me wear one of the hats and ride on the truck. As a kid, I loved everything about it. The fact they all stayed at the house together, the big dog they had, all the great equipment. And especially the excitement when the alarm went off, with everyone rushing to the truck, then the lights flashing and the siren blaring. As I got older, and realized how much more there was to it, I couldn't imagine doing anything else."

The intensity in his brown eyes reminded her of Jesse when he'd talked about the job.

"Doesn't it scare you going into a burning building?" she asked, even though she knew the answer.

"Of course," Carter said. "I'm human. But it's also a huge rush of excitement and . . . man, when you pull someone out of that fire . . ." His hands tightened into fists as his eyes shone. "It's so worth it." He gazed at her. "Most people never get a chance to save a life, or maybe once in a lifetime. We do it every single day."

Emotion welled up inside her.

"What about you, Simon?" she asked.

"I didn't have someone in the family who was a firefighter, but firefighters used to come into the restaurant run by the family of a friend of mine when I was young. They were really friendly guys and we used to listen to their stories with awe. Then one time, there was a fire in the restaurant. I wasn't there that day, but they pulled my friend and his parents out of the fire. My friend was burned, but he was alive because of those men. I knew right then that I wanted my life to have meaning like that."

"You're incredibly brave," she murmured, staring into his intense blue eyes, then shifting to Carter's brown ones.

Carter just shrugged. "As I said, I can't imagine doing anything else."

Her heart pounded in her chest, their courage and devotion moving her deeply.

She stood up and took Carter's hand. "Come on."

As he stood up, she held out her hand to Simon. He stood up and took it, then she led them into the house.

"Where are we going?" Simon asked.

"To the bedroom," she said, continuing to the stairs.

Then Simon tugged her back and she found herself in

his arms. His lips found hers and his tongue delved deep, driving her heart rate even faster.

"We don't need to go upstairs," he murmured against her mouth, then kissed her again.

"But I want—"

Simon chuckled. "I know what you want. And we can do it right here."

He tugged her into the living room and over to the couch. He sat down, pulling her onto his lap. Carter stood in front of her as Simon cupped her breasts and squeezed. She arched against him, her pulse racing. Her nipples peaked, punching into his big hands.

Carter knelt in front of her and flicked open the first button of her shirt. Then the next. Soon it was half undone and Simon was pulling it open as Carter continued down the placket. Simon's big hands cupped her lace-clad breasts and caressed, sending heat thrumming through her.

"You have beautiful breasts, sweetheart," Simon said as he nuzzled her neck.

Tingles danced down her spine.

"Thank you," she said in a daze.

Carter laughed as he pulled her now fully open shirt from her jeans. The rasping sound of the zipper as he undid it sent goose bumps dancing across her flesh.

Simon slipped her shirt from her shoulders and she pulled her arms free. He tossed it away, then she felt his hands working on the back of her bra. The elastic released and he dropped the straps from her shoulders.

She leaned back against him as he drew the cups from her breasts, then tossed the lacy garment to the floor.

Carter smiled at the sight of her naked breasts, and he covered them both with his hands. As he caressed her swollen mounds, while Simon's lips played over her collarbone, she melted into a boneless mass.

Carter's mouth covered one of her nipples and he suckled softly.

"Oh, yes. I love that," she said.

He licked it, then moved to the other. Simon covered the abandoned breast with his hand as Carter teased her nipple with his lips and tongue. Simon's fingers glided over her sensitive bud and soon she was squirming on Simon's lap, needing so much more.

She couldn't believe that she was going to experience that intense pleasure again so soon. But this time, both of them would make love to her. She would feel Carter's cock inside her today as well as Simon's.

As if sensing her need, Carter tugged on her jeans, pulling them down her thighs, then to the floor. She kicked them away, then opened her legs wide for him. She could already feel the slickness dampening her panties.

A cell phone rang. Not hers.

"That's the chief," Simon said. He pulled his phone from his pocket and answered it. He only spoke a few words, then hung up. "Sorry, bad news. They're short one guy and need one of us to come in for a few hours to cover."

Her heart pounded. Oh, God, they couldn't stop now.

"You have to go right this second?" she asked. Her voice was throaty and full of need.

Simon laughed. "Don't worry. We won't leave you high

and dry." He glanced at Carter. "I'll go. Then you and Rikki can continue what we've started here."

"You sure?" Carter asked.

"It's only fair. I got to enjoy the main event last night." Simon kissed Rikki's cheek. "Is that okay with you, Rikki?"

The thought of being alone with one of them . . . of having sex with just Carter . . . was disorienting. It would be so much more . . . intimate.

Carter's hand stroked across her belly, her skin blazing under his touch.

"Uh-huh," she breathed.

Carter smiled as he drew her to her feet. Simon kissed her, then adjusted his jeans and headed for the door.

"You two have fun," he said as he opened the door, then he turned back to them and smiled. "And think of me."

Rikki nodded, then he closed the door behind him.

She turned and stared up at Carter.

"Don't look so terrified. I know I said I was worried about going too fast last night, but I promise, I'll take it slow and easy." He hesitated. "Unless . . . you want to wait until Simon comes back."

She shook her head. "No, I just . . . ever since I met the two of you, I think of you together . . . of me being with both of you." She cupped his cheek. "But . . . I want to be with you. Now."

A slow smile spread across his face. "Okay. Well, then, come here."

He pulled her into his arms and his lips found hers. The

kiss was deep and passionate. And intensely sexy as his tongue explored her mouth thoroughly.

His hand glided over her naked back and she could feel his cock hardening under his jeans. She stroked over his shoulders, then down his chest. She began undoing the buttons on his shirt.

He released her mouth and she pressed her lips to his collarbone, feeling the rising pulse there, then kissed down his hard chest as the shirt fell open. When she reached his jeans, she tugged the shirt free then smiled up at him as she unfastened the belt, then tugged on it, pulling it from the belt loops. She tossed it to the floor, then unfastened his jeans.

She pulled down the zipper, and as the denim parted, revealing his black and charcoal–patterned boxers beneath, her heart rate accelerated. She ran her finger down the bulge under the thin fabric of his boxers. It was hard and swelling larger. She pulled down his jeans, dropping them to his ankles, then wrapped her fingers around his hidden shaft and glided her hand up and down.

He drew her into a kiss again.

"Since you like the water so much, let's go out to the hot tub."

"But the neighbors . . . ?" she protested.

Carter tugged her hand, drawing her with him to the patio doors.

"The backyard is totally private. I promise you."

Before she knew it, they were on the deck, her in just her skimpy undies and Carter in his boxers. He opened the cover, then turned on the bubbles. She watched as he dropped his boxers to the deck, revealing his big, hard cock. She couldn't help licking her lips.

"Your turn," he said with a smile.

She nodded, then pushed down her small white panties and placed them on a nearby deck chair. Carter's gaze glided up and down her naked body and she felt self-conscious.

He chuckled. "You're getting all shy on me."

"What? No," she denied.

He stepped close. "Yes, you are." He drew her against him, his arms around her waist, as he gazed down at her. "Your cheeks are all flushed."

He stroked her hair back from her face, his brown eyes glittering.

"Okay. I'm just not used to being naked in front of a man."

"Good. I don't want you naked in front of any men except me and Simon."

He cupped her face and drew her in for a kiss, his lips full and delightfully persuasive on hers. He opened and she glided her tongue inside, tentatively exploring his mouth. He held her tighter, her breasts pressed against his solid chest. Her nipples peaked, longing for the feel of his hands. His mouth.

He drew back and guided her to the edge of the tub, then held her hand as she stepped into the hot, bubbling water. He stepped in, too.

"Wait. Why don't you sit on the side?" she asked.

His eyebrow raised. "Yeah? Why?" He sat down on the

edge, his legs in the water, his grin telling her he knew exactly why.

She knelt on the seat and leaned toward him, resting one hand on his thigh.

"Because I want to do this."

Chapter Eleven

Rikki wrapped her hand around his thick, hard cock and stroked. She watched the big, bulbous head glide up and down within her grasp, pushing up past her fingers, then disappearing within their grip again. Over and over.

He got harder in her hand. And she could feel the veins pulsing.

"You like this?" she asked.

"Of course, babe. I love you touching me."

She smiled and leaned forward then pressed her lips to his tip. She kissed him, then smiled.

"Do you like being in my mouth, too?"

"Fuck, yeah."

She laughed and wrapped her lips around him, then glided down as deep as she could. He twitched in her mouth as she drew back, then with her hand firmly around him, ran her tongue over his corona, laving the entire surface thoroughly.

"Oh, yeah."

She loved the grating need in his masculine voice. She

dove down on him again, taking him deep, then she sucked on his big cock. She glided up and down, squeezing and sucking.

"Ah, fuck, baby, that's so good."

She lifted her head and gazed at his face.

He smiled. "I love seeing my cock in your mouth." He stroked her long hair back from her face. "I love feeling your soft warmth around me."

She eased down, then up again, but before she could continue, he grasped her shoulders and pressed her around as he slipped into the water. His cock fell from her mouth and she found herself sitting in one of the contoured seats, with him kneeling in front of her.

He kissed her, then murmured against her ear.

"But there's somewhere else I'm desperate to be right now."

At first, she thought he meant he was leaving, but then his hand glided down her stomach and his fingers dipped into her folds.

"Ohhhh," she murmured as he slipped inside her, his curved fingers stroking her sensitive passage.

"You're so wet." His breath fluttered against her temple. "I want to be inside you so much."

She opened her legs wider. "Me, too." Her insides ached for him.

He dipped deeper, stroking her faster.

"Oh, please." She found his cock and squeezed it, to his groan.

He wrapped his hand around his cock and pressed it to

her. The feel of him gliding it over her hot slit sent need careening through her. She wrapped her arms around him and pulled him closer.

"Please."

"Please what, baby?" His lips brushed her temple.

"I want you inside me."

"Why?" He dragged over her again, making her whimper. "Say exactly what you want, baby. I want to hear you say dirty things to me."

Excitement swelled through her at the thought.

"I want you to push your big cock inside me." Her passage twitched with the need. "I want you to fuck me."

He pressed his cock against her opening. Her heart rate increased at the feel of him there, knowing with one quick stroke, he could be all the way inside her. Stretching her barely used passage wide.

"Yeah?" He stroked back her hair, gazing into her eyes. "Tell me more."

"I want to feel it glide in deep and slow . . . filling me all the way."

"Oh, yeah." He pushed forward and his corona opened her as it moved in partway. She clung to his shoulders, wanting so much more.

But he waited.

"I want to feel it moving inside me. I want you to fuck me."

His cock slid a little deeper, his big cockhead stretching her more than Simon's had. The feel of it sent pleasure trembling through her.

But he stopped once the cockhead was inside her.

"I want to do that, baby. But first, tell me how you want it."

She squeezed around him and he moaned.

"I want you to push in all the way. Fill me with your cock."

"Yeah?"

"Then start to move inside me. Slowly at first. Then speeding up until you're fucking me deep and hard."

He pushed forward, moving slowly inside her. The feel of his erection filling her . . . stretching her tight passage . . . made her insides quiver.

His hands cupped her bottom and he pulled her tight to him, pushing his cock even deeper inside her.

"Oh, yeah," she murmured, then nipped his shoulder.

"Fuck, baby. I love that."

She nipped him again, then dragged her teeth over his skin. He tightened his grip on her bottom, pulling her even closer. He was so deep it felt like he'd push into her stomach. She squeezed around him and he groaned.

"I'm going to fuck you now, babe. But I'm going to take it slow. If I get carried away . . . or go too fast . . . just tell me."

She nodded, just wanting him to do it. She was desperate for the feel of him moving inside her.

He drew back, his cockhead stroking her sensitive passage. She moaned as he almost slipped out of her, then slowly moved forward again. She welcomed him, her intimate muscles squeezing him in a tight hug of appreciation.

When he was all the way inside her again, he kissed her

forehead. His arms tightened around her and he held her close.

"I can't believe I'm inside you, baby. That you're letting me be with you like this."

She gazed into his brown eyes, amazed at the warmth and tenderness she saw there. He was big and masculine . . . his cock deep inside her . . . and she felt so loved and protected in his embrace.

She rested her hand on his cheek, her gaze locked on his, and she kissed him. Their lips moved together, melting her heart at his gentleness.

Then he began to move.

His cock stroked her insides. Stretching her. Caressing her. It was like they were meant to be together. Their bodies designed to fit perfectly.

Sweet pleasure swelled through her as he moved inside her. Spiraling outward . . . filling her whole being. Gliding into her deeper and faster.

She gasped as he plunged in hard, reaching the deepest part of her.

"Fuck, baby. You okay?" he asked, his movements stopping as he held her tight to him. His fingers forked through her hair, cupping her head as his lips brushed against her temple.

"Oh, yeah," she whimpered. "It's incredible. Please don't stop fucking me."

She squeezed his cock inside her, an intense yearning bubbling inside her.

He chuckled, then kissed her. He rested his forehead against hers, still staring into her eyes.

"Don't worry, babe. I won't stop. I intend to make you come so hard you won't ever want my cock to be anywhere but inside you."

Then he drew back and thrust forward, making her gasp again.

He coiled his hand in her hair and drew her head back, his gaze locked on her face as he pulled back and surged forward again. The incredible pleasure swelling through her body at each thrust must surely show on her face.

He thrust again and she felt faint with delight.

He smiled, then picked up speed, surging into her fast and hard. Filling her with his thick shaft over and over again. Each time he drove into her, she sucked in air.

Now she was panting as he thrust into her like a jack-hammer. Her body vibrating with delight.

"Ohhhh, yesssss . . ." Her voice trailed off to a reedy moan, then as she clung to him, quivering on the edge of ecstasy, it turned to a wail. The sound rippling through her.

He pounded deep and hard and she gasped, then plummeted into free fall, clinging to him for support. Bliss blossomed inside her and she exploded in an earth-shattering orgasm.

As she continued to ride the wave, he drove deep and held her tight to him, then shuddered against her. His heat filled her and she moaned in joy.

They clung to each other, her head resting against his shoulder, as their breathing slowly returned to normal. Finally, he drew her head back and kissed her.

"You are incredibly special," he said as he gazed into her eyes.

And she saw the truth of it. That he really felt that way about her.

She hadn't felt cherished like this for a long time. Not since Jesse had held her in his arms so long ago.

And she'd missed the feeling.

She'd never had the chance to be with Jesse like this. And she wondered what it would have been like.

She couldn't imagine it, really. It would have been special.

But it was special being with Carter. And Simon.

Jesse was in the past. But Carter and Simon were here now.

And she knew she could fall in love with them.

She reached up and stroked Carter's hair back from his face.

She wanted to say something. To thank him for bringing her to life again. For reigniting the desire to be with a man. For filling the empty void inside her.

But she couldn't find the words.

He took her hand and kissed her palm.

"I love the way you're looking at me right now," Carter said. "And I hope you never stop."

Carter took Rikki's hand and led her to the shower. He turned on the water and pulled her under with him, then soaped up her body and stroked her all over. The feel of his slick hands gliding over her skin . . . touching every part of her . . . had her aching for him in no time.

She slid her hands around his neck and pulled him in for a kiss, then undulated her body against him as she moved her hands down his arms. She grasped his hips and pulled him tight to her, well aware of his thickening cock pressed against her belly.

"Your cock isn't where it's supposed to be." She smiled. "You remember you said I wouldn't want it anywhere but inside me?"

He groaned and pushed her back against the white-tiled wall. His fingers tested her—she arched at the feel of him stroking her folds—and when he felt the slickness, he gazed into her eyes as he pressed his cock against her opening, then slid inside.

She drew in air at the feel of his thick hardness filling her. She clung to his wet shoulders, drawing in a deep breath.

"Now fuck me fast and deep," she murmured.

He chuckled and nuzzled her neck.

"You're getting to know exactly what you like, eh, babe?"

Then he thrust in deep, pinning her to the wall. She gasped and hung on tighter.

He smiled and drew back, then thrust again.

Soon he was pounding into her, his thickness driving into her body in a steady stream of delight.

Then—just like that—she came, her ecstatic moans echoing off the tile walls of the shower stall. He groaned and thrust deeper, shuddering as he erupted inside her.

They stood there for a moment, the warm water flowing over their joined, naked bodies, their breathing labored. Finally, he drew back and smiled. He stroked her wet hair from her face.

"Why do I feel that now that your sexuality has been awakened, that it'll take two of us to keep you satisfied?"

She grinned. "Maybe you're right." Then she tipped her head and stared past him wistfully. "If Simon was here right now, I'd have another man all ready to go."

But he rocked against her and she realized that his cock, still inside her, was still hard.

Her eyes widened as she gazed into his glowing amber eyes.

"I didn't think that was possible," she said. "Once you've come."

"It's damned rare, but when a man's as turned on as I am whenever I'm with you . . ."

He captured her lips and kissed her, then suckled her lower lip into his mouth. He rocked his pelvis. As his cock moved inside her in short strokes, he murmured into her ear, "I may not come again, but I sure as hell can make you come again."

And true to his word, he soon had her wailing at the top of her lungs.

Rikki stood there feeling pampered as Carter patted her body all over with a big, fluffy blue towel. He dried every place imaginable on her.

"Maybe I don't need two men to keep me satisfied."

When Carter sent her a sharp stare, clearly worried that she was going to dump Simon from their threesome, she laughed.

"But it sure is good to know I have a spare." She ran her fingers through his damp, tousled hair as he caressed her thighs with the towel. "And, of course, there are things two of you can do with me that just one can't."

His eyebrow arched as he gazed up at her. "Like what?"

"Well, there are two of you to pay attention to different parts of me."

"Oh, yeah? What parts would those be?"

She laughed. "You really want me to talk dirty again? Can you really manage another time?"

He chuckled. "I'm sure I could rise to the challenge. But, seriously, I'm curious. What appeals to you about a threesome?"

"Besides the idea of having two hot guys willing to meet my every need?" she asked.

But his serious gaze told her he really did want to know.

He stood up and started drying himself.

"It's true that with two sets of hands . . . and two mouths . . . that you can . . . um . . . excite me in . . . um . . ."

She didn't know why she suddenly felt so flustered, especially after they'd just been so intimate. He'd even gotten her to talk dirty, something she never thought she'd be able to do. But in the heat of the moment . . . with his cock deep inside her . . .

He laughed and tossed aside the towel, then kissed her. "Yeah, I get it. Two mouths. One on each breast. Or one working your breast, the other deep in your pussy."

Heat wafted through her. She knew she'd quickly get to the point where she needed him inside her again.

She already wanted it. She wondered if she'd ever stop wanting Carter . . . or Simon . . . inside her.

"But we're also talking about two cocks. What do you think about that?"

She nodded, and practically squeaked, "It's good."

"Have you thought about what we can do with them? Together?"

She just blinked.

"What I'm getting at is that you had me in your mouth when Simon was fucking you that first time . . . and I loved that. It felt fantastic and it was generous of you to share your attention with me during such a momentous moment for you." He leaned in closer. "But that's not the only way for both of us to be inside you."

"Oh." She drew in a breath. "You're asking about . . . uh . . . you mean that one of you could be in the front while the other is . . . uh . . . in the back."

He stroked her hair from her face. "I don't know what you think about the idea of anal, but I don't want you to feel pressured. I'm bringing it up now just to get it into the open, in case you've been worrying about it."

The thought of a big cock sliding inside her back there was a bit scary. Especially Carter, since he was so much thicker than Simon. But then again, the thought of Simon filling her vagina had made her nervous at first. Now she had taken him on and it had been the most delightful experience of her life, and since then she'd had Carter's even thicker girth pounding into her until she exploded in bliss.

He kissed her. "I don't want an answer about it. I just want you to relax and know that we won't take that step until you want us to. If you do at all."

She nodded, then wrapped her hands around his head and pulled his face close, then kissed him thoroughly, her tongue claiming his mouth with bold strokes.

"Now, what are we going to do until Simon gets back?" she asked.

"How about a swim, then we just relax around the pool?"

"Great idea." She gathered up her clothes and followed him from the bathroom into his bedroom and dropped them on the bed. "Oh, wait, I don't have a bathing suit."

He chuckled. "You're kidding, right?"

"No. I didn't even know you had a pool, let alone that I was coming over here, when you stopped by this morning."

"I mean, you don't need a bathing suit."

He meant they'd go skinny-dipping.

"I'm sorry, I'm not really comfortable with the idea of running around naked in the backyard."

He ran his hand over her hip and dragged his gaze down her body. "You were naked in the hot tub."

"I know but . . . spending a couple of hours out there . . . naked. What if Simon comes back and brings someone with him? Or someone shows up? Or—"

He stopped her words with a kiss, then laughed. "You worry too much. But if you really want a bathing suit, I have something for you."

As he walked across the bedroom then out the door, she couldn't help admiring his tight, sexy butt. He returned a moment later with something brightly colored in his hand, then tossed it on the bed.

She stared at the small scraps of shocking pink, lemon, and neon green floral fabric.

"One of the guys at the firehouse gave it to me as a joke. There was a running gag that under my uniform, I'm always wearing a man-kini. So one of the guys left this in my locker. Don't know why I kept it, but I'm glad I did."

She lifted the bottoms, which basically consisted of a string attached to a small triangle. And the top was two triangles.

"I'm not sure this is better than naked," she said, staring at it.

He grinned. "That's why I gave it to you."

Her cheeks flushed.

He sat down. "Seriously though, I'd love to see you in that. And don't worry. If someone other than Simon were to show up—which they won't—you can just wrap a towel around yourself. They wouldn't think anything of it."

"I guess."

She leaned over and stepped into the bikini bottoms, then pulled them up and positioned the triangle in place. She wasn't used to wearing thongs, so the string in her butt felt strange.

As she wrapped the top around her body and struggled with the clasp, he caught her hips and turned her away from him.

"Let me help with that." He fastened the clasp then drew her hair to one side so she could tie the string at her neck.

"You just wanted to see my butt."

His fingers lightly danced over one round cheek.

"I'm not going to lie. I *love* seeing your butt."

At the feel of his lips playing over her ass, delightful tingles danced through her. Then he slapped it.

"Okay, let's get going."

Rikki and Carter spent the next couple of hours swimming and sunning themselves. They talked about how she'd been laid off from her job, and bounced ideas around about what she might do next.

The fire department shoot had made her realize how much fun she had doing photography, and she and Carter brainstormed ways she could turn it into a full-time business.

That was another thing she liked about Carter. He was a lighthearted guy who liked to laugh, but he was also incredibly smart. He even offered to help her build a Web site to showcase her work.

Finally, as the afternoon shadows grew long, they returned to the house.

She was going to change, but Carter tossed her a T-shirt and suggested she just pull that on. While she did, he checked his phone and said that Simon would still be a couple of hours. They decided to wait to start dinner.

"Let's watch a movie," he suggested.

"Sounds good."

He sat down on the couch and she settled in beside him. He offered several movie choices, but she told him to take his pick. He put on an action movie and she soon found herself dozing in his arms.

A sound startled her and she opened her eyes. The TV was off and she realized that there had been the blaring sounds of a high-speed chase a moment ago.

"I didn't mean to wake you."

Chapter Twelve

Rikki glanced in the direction of Simon's voice. He stood off to her right by the armchair with the remote control in his hand.

She pushed the hair from her face and smiled. "That's okay."

"You two look cozy." He smiled. "Have a good afternoon?"

From the sound of deep breathing beside her, she knew Carter was still asleep.

"Yeah, we went in the hot tub, then spent the afternoon by the pool."

"That sounds like much more fun than putting out a fire in a newspaper stand." He smiled, appreciatively gazing at her naked legs curled in front of her. "Especially if it involved watching you skinny-dipping."

"No, afraid not. Got a bathing suit on under this shirt."

"Yeah? You want to show me?"

She realized she did.

She glanced at the still sleeping Carter and eased herself away, then stood up. Excitement sizzled through her at Simon's heated gaze locked on her when she moved toward him. She peeled the shirt from her body and tossed it aside, her hormones twitching as his blue eyes darkened to navy at the sight of her barely covered breasts.

She flattened her hands on his chest and pressed him backward to the armchair, then pushed him into it. She climbed onto his lap and unbuttoned his shirt. The feel of his hard, sculpted muscles under her fingertips aroused her.

"You feel good," she murmured as she kissed his neck.

She felt his hands slide under her breasts and lift.

"So do you." His thumbs glided over her nipples and they surged forward.

Oh, God, she didn't know what had gotten into her, but his touch triggered a lightning response. Her insides ached with a desperate need for him. To feel him inside her. To ride him to a sudden, stupendous release that would take both their breaths away.

She pulled aside the scraps of fabric covering her breasts so that he was touching her bare skin. He chuckled, then covered one nipple with his mouth. She moaned softly as he suckled her, her fingers tearing at the button holding his jeans closed, then tugging down the zipper.

She reached inside and grasped his cock, arching her breast against his hungry mouth. When she freed his long shaft, she stroked it, feeling it swell and lengthen in her hand until it was rock-hard.

"Oh, fuck, sweetheart, I missed you."

"Me, too." She whimpered as he suckled hard on her nub again. "Oh, God, I want you inside me."

She tugged aside the fabric covering her intimate folds, and positioned herself over him. When she pressed his cock-head against her wetness, he moaned. Then his tongue swirled over her needy nipple.

She lowered herself onto him, taking the entire length of him into her aching canal. When she finally rested against him, her body totally impaled, both of them sucked in air.

"Damn, sweetheart, this is one hell of a welcome home."

She leaned in and kissed his neck, rocking her pelvis. He groaned.

"What can I say?" she said in a husky voice. "I missed you."

He chuckled. "Don't tell me Carter couldn't keep you satisfied."

She nuzzled his neck, then kissed along his collarbone, continuing to rock slightly. Enough to keep a raging fire burning inside her.

"Oh, he satisfied me all right. Enough to make me re-alize what I've been missing all these years. And how much I want to make up for it."

She realized that Carter might wake up at any time. Might even be awake now. Watching them. The thought shot her arousal up several notches.

She widened her legs around Simon and rocked forward again, pushing him deeper inside her.

"Well, halle-fucking-lujah for Carter." Simon groaned. "You've certainly gotten the knack of this."

Then he grasped her hips and guided her. Rocking her faster. And deeper.

She moaned at the feel of his long cock gliding within her.

"Oh, God, I'm close already," she murmured. And then began to moan as heat pulsed through her.

His cock stroked her faster and faster and her insides quivered in excitement. She rested her hands on his big shoulders and gripped tightly as she started moving on him in earnest. Sliding his granite-hard erection in and out of her. She slowed for a few strokes, then sped up, then slowed again, garnering a deep moan from him.

Then she quickened her pace again. Taking him in and out. Riding him like a wild stallion, her pulse skyrocketing. Pleasure pummeled her insides and she threw her head back and began to wail as bliss surged through her.

He rocked his hips with hers, their bodies pounding together. She gasped as he pumped deeper into her, then moaned as the orgasm blossomed through her. Her trilling voice filled the room. He stroked her clit and her whole consciousness exploded in an overwhelming cataclysm of joy.

She seemed to float in eternity, riding a wave of euphoria. Then she slowly drifted back to earth, finding herself trembling in his arms. His lips caressed her temple, her head tucked under his chin.

"Oh, God . . . that was . . ." she panted, ". . . incredible."

He stroked her hair, then rested his hand over her ear, holding her head to his chest. His heart was beating double-time.

"It was that," he said.

Finally, she lifted her head and gazed up at him. He smiled and captured her lips.

"And I nearly slept through it," Carter said from across the room.

She gazed around to see him sitting up on the couch where she'd left him, his cock in his hand, deflated and glistening. It seemed he'd enjoyed her and Simon's encounter from afar.

"It's too bad. If you'd held back, we could have entertained Simon with another round."

Carter grinned. "Oh, believe me, with even the tiniest help from you, I can be *up* and ready in no time."

"Did you enjoy Carter watching you, sweetheart?" Simon murmured against her ear, then kissed it.

She shifted on Simon's lap, pleasure quivering through her at the feel of his semi-erect cock still inside her. She squeezed him, then groaned when he twitched.

Her voice came out hoarse when she said, "I think maybe I did."

Rikki sipped the cold beer Carter handed her, sitting back in the chair as Simon placed a piece of the gooey, outrageously delicious-smelling pizza onto her plate. She picked it up and took a bite.

"Oh, my God, you're right. This is the best pizza I've ever tasted," she said.

"Told you," Simon said. "It's a little family place just around the corner. Everything's made from scratch."

"And I'm sure they double up the cheese and toppings for us," Carter said as he grabbed a slice for himself.

"And always throw in free cookies. Wait until you taste those."

"We put out a fire in their place about a year ago," Simon explained. "We won't let them give us the pizza for free, so they do that instead."

"It must be nice to know you help people," she said. "That restaurant. The people whose lives you saved. You touch the lives of people around here every day."

"That's why we do it," Carter said.

She nodded. Jesse had told her the same thing.

"So have you ever lost a fellow firefighter?" she found herself asking.

Carter frowned. "Yeah, about four years ago. One of the guys we went through training with."

She nodded sympathetically. "So how did you deal with it?"

Simon pulled at the label on his beer bottle, pulling the edge up.

"It isn't easy," he said. "You just get on with your life."

"We knew that he'd want us to keep on doing what we're doing. Saving lives. Helping people. That's what it's all about," Carter added.

"Do you ever talk about it?" Rikki asked.

Carter shrugged. "What's the point? These things happen. It's part of the job."

"You've got to remember," Simon said somberly, "we face danger every single day. Every one of us knows it. It's painful to lose one of our own, but there's nothing we can do about it. It's part of who we are. Of what we do."

Her heart ached. "So you just keep the pain inside?"

An uncomfortable silence fell and Rikki regretted bringing up the subject.

Finally, Carter changed the subject and they continued eating.

When they finished dinner, they played some cards. As they were laughing over a joke Carter told, Rikki felt her cell buzz. She pulled it from her jeans pocket and glanced at it.

"Sorry, I'm going to take this. It's from a friend back home." She pressed the button and held the phone to her ear. "Cindy, how are you doing?"

"Hi. I'm fine. How are you finding it there? Do you like your new place?"

Cindy worked at the firehouse where Jesse had been stationed. They kept in touch and used to run together a couple of times a week before Rikki had moved.

"It's good. My roommates are working out."

"That's great. The reason I'm calling is because Tony asked if I'd give him your phone number. He's going to be passing by there on a trip to visit his parents, so he wanted to call you to get together. Is that okay?"

Her chest tightened. Tony was one of Jesse's friends. She'd gotten to know him pretty well when she used to hang out with them on their days off.

"Uh . . . sure. That would be fine. Thanks for asking."

They chatted a little longer, then Rikki hung up.

"What was that?" Simon asked. "Everything okay?"

She slipped her phone back in her pocket.

"Uh, yeah. A friend's going to be passing through town and wants to visit me."

"That's nice," Carter said.

She just nodded distractedly.

Simon dealt another hand, then he watched Rikki with concern as she spread out her cards and gazed at them. Something was bothering her.

They played another couple of hands and Simon wound up winning, even though Rikki had been ahead. He could tell her head wasn't in the game.

He pushed the deck of cards aside and stood up, then offered his hand.

"Let's go in the living room," he suggested.

She took his hand and followed him. He sat down on the couch and she sat beside him. Carter sat on her other side.

Simon squeezed her hand. "Ever since that phone call, you've been distracted. Why don't you tell us what's going on?"

She frowned. "It's nothing, really. I just . . ." She shrugged. "I guess I just started thinking about Ashton and the life I left behind and . . ." She pushed her hair back, but he was pretty sure she was actually dashing away a tear.

At her hesitation, Carter prompted, "Whatever it is, you can tell us."

She nodded. "I know but . . . you don't really want to hear this."

"Try us," Simon coaxed.

She sighed. "I just started thinking that . . . in leaving Ashton, I've left Jesse behind, too."

"That's a good thing." Carter took her other hand. "I

don't mean leaving behind good memories of him, or for-
getting how you felt about him, but it is good for you to
finally move on."

She nodded. "Yeah, I know. It's just . . . It still hurts.
Thinking of him. Remembering how he died." Her
eyes welled with tears. "I'll never forget when Chief Rogers
showed up at my door to tell me." She shook her head. "I
never want to feel that kind of pain again." She gazed up at
Simon with imploring eyes.

He squeezed her hand again. "I know, sweetheart. I
can't imagine what you went through."

"Look, I don't want you to get the wrong impression,"
she said. "What the three of us are sharing is fun and exciting, but—"

"No, don't add a 'but' to that sentence," Simon said. He
knew where this was going.

"I can't let you think that . . . there'll ever be any
more . . . to this relationship . . . than that." She spoke
slowly, taking calming breaths along the way.

"This is not a casual fling," Carter said. "What we have
is deeper than that."

She shook her head. "No. I can't. I told you that right
from the beginning."

Simon slid his arm around her and drew her close.

"You've just been thrown off balance getting that call
from your friend. We can work this out. We can help you
past this."

"No. I . . ." She sucked in a breath and stared at him
with a resolute expression. "I think we should end this before we get any more deeply involved."

His heart clenched.

"Rikki, I know you suffered a great deal. But there are no guarantees you won't get hurt again. That you won't lose someone you love, no matter what they do for a living."

"But the odds with firefighters—"

"Are higher. Granted. But that doesn't mean you should walk away from what we have." He smiled. "Which is fantastic, by the way."

The glitter of tears in her eyes tore at his heart. She was in pain, and he knew if she fell for them, like he was falling for her, and he knew Carter was, too, that she would be on tenterhooks every day worrying about losing them. But that didn't mean she should run away. She had to find the strength inside herself to make this work. Because otherwise she would never find true happiness.

He stroked her hair behind her ear, and cradled her head in his hands, then kissed her. Her lips were soft and pliable under his.

"Rikki, you don't have to make a commitment right now. All we ask is that you give this relationship a chance. Go into it with the belief that it could work out between us."

She gazed at him, shaking her head. "I shouldn't," she murmured. "It'll only get harder."

"All I can say is that, for me," Simon said, "walking away from you right now would be impossible. I need to see where this might go. Don't you?"

She glanced from him to Carter. Carter tugged her close and captured her lips. She sank back on the couch as he deepened the kiss. Simon could see their mouths moving.

See her melt into Carter's embrace. When his friend released her and the two of them gazed into each other's eyes, she seemed captivated.

"Give us a chance, baby," Carter insisted.

She drew in a deep breath. The next few moments hung between them for what seemed like an eternity. Simon felt as if he couldn't breathe.

Then finally Rikki nodded.

"Okay," she murmured.

During the next shift at the firehouse, Simon rounded everyone up and helped Rikki get organized to start doing the photo shoot. It was a beautiful, sunny day, so she set up outside with the firehouse in the background.

The first two in line were Tanner and Kyle.

Tanner, the tall Texan, strolled into position, then pulled off his T-shirt. The sight of his broad chest and ridged ab muscles made her think of Simon and Carter as she'd watched them strip off their shirts this morning and drag her off to the shower with them.

He put on his fire hat and she snapped pictures of him posing in different ways. She didn't need to direct him. He was a natural in front of the camera. He grabbed different pieces of equipment and used them in a creative, yet natural way. Like holding an axe crossed in front of his body, throwing a coiled fire hose over his shoulder, and carrying one of the big power saws at his side. Sometimes he'd stand, sometimes he'd walk, his gaze intent, as if he were actually walking into a fire.

Except for the fact that he was bare-chested.

Kyle was up next and he was a little uncertain, so she gave him directions. Only the six men they'd scheduled for the morning session were around watching and waiting their turn, but they started giving suggestions and she wound up taking some shots of several of them together. Leaning on the truck as if taking a break, some action shots of them running or walking with intense stares, and a few with them getting out of the truck.

Some of these would be great as promo photos.

"Get some good shots this morning?" Carter asked as she sat down beside him at the table in the firehouse kitchen, a plate in her hand.

Simon joined them, as did Tanner and a couple of others from the morning's shoot.

"Yes. The guys were really great to work with. They had some good suggestions and we got a lot of extra photos that could be used for the calendar cover and promo images. I also thought that it might be a good idea to put together a Web site and social media pages specifically to promote the calendar. All these extra photos would be useful for that."

"I'm not sure we have the resources for a Web site," Simon said.

"I'd be happy to volunteer to design and develop it. It would be helpful to me to hone those skills for the work I'll do with Cassie. So then it'll just be hosting charges for the Web site, and you should be able to cover that small amount with sales from the calendar."

"Sold," Simon said.

She ate the chicken enchilada as the men turned the conversation to small talk. After lunch, Carter explained that they couldn't spare most of the men she needed for the afternoon shoot because an expert who was supposed to come and give them some training next shift had to switch to today.

"We don't need Dodge, though, so you can do him," Carter said as the other men headed out the door.

"Yes, you can definitely do me."

She turned at the sound of Dodge's voice to see the tall, tattooed fireman leaning against the doorway, a slow smile spreading across his face.

Carter sent Dodge a warning gaze, then he squeezed her arm. "See you later."

She and Carter and Simon had decided not to let people at the firehouse know about their relationship. Not yet. But Carter was definitely acting protective. Hopefully, it just came across as a lieutenant's concern for a visitor to the firehouse.

Carter went outside with the others and Dodge stepped closer.

"You and Carter got something going on?" Dodge asked.

"No, nothing like that."

She could look out for herself, so she didn't need to make it look like she was under Carter's protection. Anyway, Dodge might have an unmistakable bad-boy vibe, with his tattooed arms, defiant blue eyes, and definite swagger, but she also sensed that he was a strong, protective type himself.

He nodded. "We can't take shots outside like you did this morning, since that'll get in the way of the training exercises. So what do you have in mind?"

"There's good natural light in the living area with those big windows, but it's not great as a backdrop. Maybe it'll be better to just wait until the drills are finished."

"That's okay by me, but then, there are those other shots you wanted to do."

"Other shots?"

"Yeah, for your portfolio. Didn't you say you could sell them to make book covers?"

"Oh. I think I'll have a lot from the photos I already have."

"I thought you wanted some that were . . . sexier. Cassie says that some of her author clients write some pretty steamy stuff. Won't they want something different from what you've got for the calendar?"

Chapter Thirteen

Rikki pursed her lips. He was right.

"Okay, I guess we could do that."

A slow smile spread across his face. "I have the perfect place for them."

He turned and headed to the stairs. She followed him up to the second floor, quivering with nerves at the thought of being alone with the tall, uber-masculine man, especially around so many beds.

He strolled into one of the rooms and walked to the bed near the window, then he turned and pulled off his T-shirt, revealing more tattoos across his chest. In fact, most of his torso was inked. But not so much to hide all the natural color of his tanned skin.

He pulled back the cover on the bed, then sat down. With a smile, he stretched out and tucked his hands behind his head.

"What are you doing?" she asked nervously, worried his move was an invitation to join him.

"I'm getting into a sexy pose for you." He grinned. "Here, is this better?"

He unbuttoned his pants, then pulled the zipper down enough so she could see the top of his navy boxers. The sight of the dusting of curly hair forming an arrow down to his boxers—then him shifting the boxers down a little more, revealing more male groin that she was comfortable with—had her breath quickening. Before something embarrassing popped into view, he pulled the sheet over him. He arranged it so that it was low on his hips and looked like he was naked in the bed, with an enticing amount of male flesh showing to make the pose intensely sexy.

Oh, God, this was going to be an incredible series of shots.

Putting aside her discomfort, she grabbed her camera and started taking pictures. As they continued, he changed the draping of the sheet, shifted the position of his arms, changed his expression from brooding, to sexy, to smoldering.

"Those were some great shots," she said finally, lowering her camera. "The tattoos make them especially sexy."

He grinned. "Glad to be of service."

He tossed aside the covers and she dragged her gaze from his open pants. Everything was covered, but the whole situation just felt . . . intimate.

He stood up and, to her relief, pulled up the zipper, then he walked toward her.

"There are other shots we can do, too," he said as he moved close, his masculine aura rippling across her awareness. He rested his hands on her upper arms and drew her in closer. "Why don't you put the camera on automatic and take some shots?"

But she knew he didn't care so much about the pictures as he leaned toward her, clearly intending to kiss her.

"This is not a good idea," she said.

"I disagree." His mouth surged to hers and his persuasive lips seared her.

She quickly pulled back, but not before Simon appeared in the doorway.

"What the hell is going on?" he demanded.

Dodge turned and assessed the angry glower on Simon's face and Rikki's wide-eyed expression.

"Fuck, sorry, Lieutenant. I didn't realize the two of you were involved."

"We're trying to keep it quiet while Rikki's doing her work here," Simon said. "But I'm sure you'll understand that I expect you to keep your hands off."

"Of course, sir." Dodge glanced at her and nodded. "And, sir. Rikki wasn't a part of it. I caught her off guard. That's all."

He grabbed his shirt and pulled it on.

"Fine. And Dodge . . ." Simon said. "Button up your pants."

Dodge tucked in his shirt and fastened the button, then headed down the stairs. As Simon approached Rikki, her stomach soured, tensing with his every step forward.

"I'm really sorry, Simon."

He moved in close and tipped up her chin. "Why?"

She stared into his intense blue eyes. Was that a challenge? To get her to inventory what she'd done wrong? How she'd betrayed both him and Carter?

She shook her head. "About what you just saw," was all she could manage to say.

"Dodge just told me he caught you off guard. Was that a lie? Did you intend to kiss him?"

"No, of course not, but . . ." She sucked in a breath. "I shouldn't have let it happen."

"So you're going to take responsibility for him making a move on you?"

She pursed her lips. "I . . . well, no."

He smiled. "Then don't worry about it. You're a beautiful woman. Men are going to hit on you. As long as you say no, that's all that's important."

Then he cupped her head and planted his mouth on hers. His tongue teased her lips and she opened, then he swept inside. Soon she was melting into him.

Then he drew back. "Except me and Carter, of course."

"Hmm. What?" she asked in a daze.

He chuckled. "I said to say no to men who hit on you, except me and Carter."

She smiled. "Okay, it's a deal."

"So how are my favorite guys in the world?"

Rikki glanced up from her laptop at the sound of Cassie's voice. The handful of men relaxing in the sitting area on break greeted her as she walked across the living area to where Rikki sat at the desk in the corner.

Rikki had gone through the photos she'd taken so far and identified several for each of the first few months of the calendar, as well as a selection of others she thought might be useful for promotion.

Cassie sat down beside her and gave her a hug, then glanced at the screen. Rikki walked through the photos for the first two month slots, then the action shots.

"Oh, those are really good," Cassie said. "I especially love the one with Kyle leaning against the truck."

"We always knew he was your favorite," Tanner called out.

Cassie laughed. "Oh, Kyle is pretty special, but you know you're all my favorites. And, Tanner, that one of you with the axe in your hand and that fierce expression on your face looking like you're going to take on the world . . ." She smiled. "Very sexy."

While they went through the other photos for the months Rikki had so far, the alarm sounded. The men rushed out. Rikki watched as Simon and Carter hurried after them. Carter glanced back and their gazes met. She sent him her please-be-careful look and he nodded, then disappeared out the door.

Rikki continued showing Cassie the additional photos she'd taken, while telling her about the idea of setting up a Web site and social media and how she suggested they use the pictures. Cassie thought it was a great idea and that it would be good experience for more work that she could do for Cassie's clients.

Finally, Rikki shut the computer and suggested they grab some dinner. Instead of going out, they ordered in a pizza—Rikki suggested the place they'd tried the other night—and they sat back at the table and enjoyed their pizza and sodas.

"Sooo," Cassie said, gazing at Rikki speculatively. "What was that when Carter was heading out the door? I sensed a little magic there. Have things progressed with you and him?"

"Uh . . . yeah."

Cassie smiled. "Oh, really? And what about Simon?"

Rikki nodded.

Cassie gripped her arm. "Seriously? You've been with both of them? Was that at the same time, or you're just seeing both of them?"

Rikki couldn't help but laugh at the glittering delight in Cassie's eyes.

"That's pretty personal stuff."

"Come on, Rikki. Just spill the beans. I've always told you all my sexual secrets. Don't torture me with suspense. I want details."

"Okay, fine. I was with them. Both. At the same time."

"I thought so! You lucky thing. So how was it?"

"It was . . ." She was going to say great and leave it at that, but she knew Cassie would push her for more and . . . well, Cassie was her best friend. If she couldn't talk to her, who could she talk to?

"Yes?"

Rikki sighed. "Cassie, there's something I've never told you."

Cassie's smile faded at Rikki's serious tone.

"When I was going out with Jesse, I'd never been with a man."

"I knew that. You told me how young you were and that you and he were waiting for your eighteenth birthday."

"And that he died three weeks before that."

Cassie's hand rested on hers. "Yes. I know it was horrendous for you."

Rikki just nodded. "Well, what I didn't tell you is that . . . after Jesse died, I just couldn't bring myself to . . ." She shrugged. "Move on."

"I know you were reluctant to get serious about anyone because of Jesse."

"No, not just that. I mean . . . I never . . . I mean, the idea of being with a man after that . . . It just felt wrong. I dated from time to time, but it never led to anything serious . . . or physical."

"You mean, you never . . . ?"

Rikki shook her head.

"So you're a virgin? I mean . . . you were?"

"Yes. Until Simon and Carter."

"Oh, my God. So you gave up your virginity to . . . both of them? How does that even work?"

"They each gave me a first."

Cassie's face split into a grin. "Oh, my God, you *bad* girl."

Rikki suddenly realized exactly what Cassie thought. The same thing Carter had discussed with her the other night, when he'd said he didn't want her to feel pressured to be with both of them—front and back—at the same time.

Now Cassie gazed at Rikki with admiration, like she was her hero.

"Now you've made me want to be more adventurous. I've never had a threesome before, not outside my fantasies anyway." Cassie grinned broadly. "I would think Dodge and Tanner would be an incredible combination. Tanner's so charming, and Dodge . . ." She rested her hand on her chest. "Well, those tattoos! And his take-charge attitude."

Rikki laughed. "I think I created a monster."

"So you're just having fun and keeping it light, right? I know you didn't want to get involved with firefighters."

"That's what I intended originally but what we have is so great . . . They asked me to give the relationship a chance, and I agreed."

Cassie's smile faded. "Oh sweetie, this isn't going to end well."

"Why would you say that? I thought you told me to open up and see where things lead?"

"Okay, let's get serious here." Cassie's expression turned no-nonsense. "You're having sex with two guys at the same time. A threesome. There's no way that's going to work out in the long run. Someone's going to get jealous . . . possessive . . . whatever. And they're friends. So there's no way everyone's going to walk away from this unscathed. If it was just a few rounds in the hay, then sure. But a relationship?" Cassie took her hand. "You have to know that can't be good for any of you."

She squeezed Rikki's fingers. "Look, I think you're just feeling there's a deep connection because of the situation.

They were your first lovers, so you think you have special feelings for them. But that doesn't mean love. Or even anything serious. And they're probably just feeling protective of you, since I assume they know it was your first time."

Rikki nodded.

"So you see? You're all just caught up in that. But you might want to stick with the plan to keep it light and casual. You don't want to put yourself back in the position where you're living with fear every time they go out on a call."

"Like they are right now." Rikki shrugged. "It happens so often I'm getting used to it."

She didn't admit that it still worried her every time she heard the siren and they swarmed out.

"Thanks for your concern," Rikki said, "but it's complicated and I need to figure this out on my own."

Cassie squeezed her hand. "I know. I just don't want to see you hurt again."

Rikki heard the truck return, then the men began to file into the house, their expressions grim. Instantly, Rikki filled with anxiety.

"What's happened?" she asked when she saw Tanner and Dodge come in. She hadn't yet seen Carter and Simon and she was sure she'd heard someone mention the hospital.

"It was a tough one. It was a warehouse fire and several people were trapped inside the building," Tanner said.

Oh, God, she didn't like where this was going. She glanced at the door. There was still no sign of Carter or Simon. Her chest clenched.

"Was one of the men hurt?" she asked, praying he'd say no.

"Yes," Dodge said. "The chief called us out, because the structure was too unstable, but Simon and Kyle had found a woman trapped and were trying to get her free."

"Oh, God." Her knees were weak and she sucked in air.

"Part of the roof collapsed and a beam fell on Kyle."

"No!" She sucked in a breath. "Is he all right? And what about Simon?"

The thought of Kyle hurt or . . . worse . . . made her ache inside. And she hated herself that she was actually relieved it was him and not Simon.

"It's okay," Tanner assured her. "Simon is fine. And Kyle is at the hospital, but it looks like it's just a broken rib. He'll be off work for a while, but he'll be okay."

"Thank God."

Then she saw Carter and Simon enter the house. She couldn't help herself. She raced toward them, then threw her arms around Simon.

"Oh, my God, I'm so glad you're all right."

He tightened his arms around her and squeezed.

"I'm all right, too," Carter said.

She slid from Simon's arms and hugged Carter.

"I heard about Kyle. I'm so sorry he got hurt," she said.

Carter tightened his arms around her.

"He did, but he'll be okay," Carter said.

She nodded and as she stepped away from Carter, Simon drew her toward him again, locking gazes with her.

"Rikki, it's part of the job. Sometimes we get hurt. But

Kyle will be back on the job after his ribs have mended. And Carter and I are both fine."

She nodded, relieved they were both here, healthy and in one piece.

But if anything had happened to them . . . if one of them had wound up dead . . . The pain that lanced through her at that thought was almost unbearable.

Carter and Simon had headed to the shower to clean up and when they got out, Rikki was waiting for them in their room. She'd left Cassie at the laptop to go through the photos and narrow down which ones to use for the calendar.

As soon as the men stepped into the room, Rikki threw her arms around Simon.

"I'm so glad you're all right." She pushed up on her tippy toes and kissed him.

He drew her tight to his warm, still slightly damp body, a towel slung carelessly at his waist. She wanted to whip it away, then tackle him onto the bed and stroke his cock until it was stiff and ready, then ride him to heaven.

Then do the same thing with Carter.

She slipped from Simon's arms and threw her arms around Carter.

"You, too. I can't bear the thought of anything happening to either of you."

She kissed Carter and his hands cupped her bottom, pulling her tighter to his body. She could feel the swell of his rigid cock.

"Baby, you're making it awfully hard for us to go downstairs and get back to work," Carter murmured against her ear, then nipped her earlobe. Tingles danced down her spine.

She stroked her fingers through his hair.

"Can't we stay up here a little while?" She smiled seductively and pressed her body tight to his rising cock.

Simon laughed as he stepped close behind her and curled his hand around her waist.

"You really are trying to make up for lost time." Simon nuzzled her neck, sending heat washing through her. "But the men are waiting for us. We had some drills planned."

"And I thought you had plans with Cassie tonight," Carter said.

She stroked one hand over Simon's raspy cheek and the other through Carter's hair.

"Cassie will understand," she said, her words coming out husky.

"Okay, you little nymph." Simon drew her from Carter and turned her around, then captured her lips. "You're soft and sweet," he said with a smile, "and definitely alluring, but as much as we'd like to do this with you right now, it'll have to wait until after shift."

He kissed her again. "So you go out with Cassie, have fun, and we'll pick you up in the morning. Then we can do whatever you like all day long."

She laughed and ran her hand down Simon's hard, muscular chest. "Mmm. All day long sounds just perfect."

Cassie and Rikki went out to dinner and a movie. She'd wanted to go see Kyle in the hospital in between, but he'd already been released. After Cassie dropped her off at home,

Rikki went right to bed, trying not to think about Simon and Carter going out on a call overnight.

But then morning came and there was a knock at the door.

"Hey in there," Tina said. "Your two sexy firefighters are at the door."

Rikki leaped out of bed and began pulling on her clothes. "Tell them I'll be right there."

Five minutes later, she raced down the stairs. Simon and Carter sat in the living room, Tina flirting with them outrageously. But when they glanced up at Rikki, their eyes glowed at the sight of her.

"I'm sorry. My alarm didn't go off."

Simon stood up. "No problem. There's nowhere else we have to be."

Carter stood, too, and she followed them to the entrance.

Tina grinned at her as she went out the door.

"Have fun," Tina called after them.

Once they arrived at the men's house, Carter opened the door and she followed them inside.

"How's Kyle?" she asked. "He's home now, right?"

"He's staying at his sister's for a while, until he can get around better," Carter explained.

"But that's not really what you want to talk about right now," Simon said as he pulled her to him.

She stroked his whisker-roughened cheek. "True. In fact, talk isn't what I had in mind at all."

She pressed her hand to the front of his pants and

squeezed, feeling his cock rise within her grip. She laughed, then stepped back and peeled off her T-shirt.

Then she turned her back to them and undid her jeans as she walked into the living room. She dropped them to the floor, then turned back to them in just her bra and panties.

The men were right behind her, shedding clothes as they went. They were in just their boxers now.

Oh, God, both their cocks were thick, hard columns. It never failed to amaze her that she had that effect on them.

"So are you two big strong firefighters here to rescue me?"

"Of course, ma'am." Carter stepped closer. "We'll do whatever it takes to keep you safe."

He scooped her up and she wrapped her arms around his neck.

"Are you going to take me outside now?" She glanced to the patio doors.

"Of course, ma'am." Carter carried her to the doors, then out onto the wooden deck. Simon preceded them down the stairs to the patio.

Carter set her down on the hot stone.

"You'll be safe here, ma'am," he said.

She smiled as she reached behind herself and unhooked her bra, watching the heat building in their eyes. The elastic loosened around her ribs and she drew the straps down, but held the bra to her chest.

"I want to thank you both," she murmured, then dropped the bra to the ground.

Chapter Fourteen

Both men's gazes locked on Rikki's naked breasts, watching her nipples peak under their intense stares.

She stepped to Carter. She pulled the elastic of his boxers forward and down enough to reveal his cockhead, then she leaned forward and kissed it.

The feel of his hot flesh against her lips sent heat fluttering through her. She dragged her tongue over the tip, teasing him for a few seconds, then she turned to Simon and did the same thing.

When she stood up again, they both stared at her like starving men ready to devour her.

She laughed then stripped off her panties and tossed them aside.

"I'll do anything you want."

Simon's eyes gleamed. "First, I want you thoroughly wet."

Oh, man, with him looking at her like that, she was already getting wet.

Both men dropped their boxers and kicked them away,

then marched toward her. But instead of pulling her into their arms, they each grabbed an arm and walked her backward toward the pool. A second later, she was falling through the air, then into the cool water.

She sputtered as she surfaced. Both of them closed in on her and guided her to the side of the pool.

She laughed as she pushed her hair back from her face. "Well, I'm definitely wet now."

"Prove it," Carter said, then he lifted her onto the side of the pool.

Water dribbled down her body, glistening in the morning sunshine.

She widened her legs and opened her folds with her fingers. Her stomach quivered at so boldly showing them her intimate flesh, but their glowing masculine gazes had her practically panting in need.

"I can't really tell," Simon said and he pulled her closer to the edge, so her butt was perched on the very side of the pool. Then Simon dragged his fingertip over her slick flesh.

"Mmm. That's good," he said. "But I want you wetter."

"I can fix that," Carter said as he pressed her legs wider and leaned forward.

First, he brushed his fingertips over her, just like Simon had done. Then his fingers dipped into her passage and he stroked, making her moan.

"She is pretty wet," Carter said, "but this will make sure."

His mouth covered her slick folds and she groaned. His tongue lapped over her slit, teasing the petals of flesh, then gliding inside her. As he swirled and licked, her fingers coiled in his wavy hair.

He drew back, to her murmur of protest, but then Simon leaned in and licked her. His hands flattened on her inner thighs, pressing her legs a little wider, then he pressed his mouth deeper into her. His lips massaged her tender flesh as his tongue worked over her opening, drilling deep, then swirling. Then it glided along her slit and found her clit.

She arched as he dabbed at it with the tip of his tongue, but his hands held her tight to the warm stone of the deck. He licked and suckled her button, flooding her with intense pleasure.

As Simon continued licking and teasing her, Carter pulled himself from the pool and crouched behind her. His hands covered her breasts and he squeezed her nipples between his fingertips. She leaned back, resting her head against his shoulder.

Simon's tongue continued to wreak havoc on her senses as Carter moved back, laying her on the warm stone. Then he leaned over her and pressed his mouth to her aching breast, taking the nipple into his mouth.

As both men sucked on her, her body churned with rising need. Pleasure coiled deep in her belly, tighter and tighter like a spring, until she could barely stand it. Carter suckled her other breast, teasing the first with his fingers. Simon glided a big finger inside her, stroking her channel as his tongue fluttered over her clit.

"Oh, God, I'm going to come."

Simon's mouth disappeared and she groaned, then he was standing over her, dripping wet, and pulled her to her feet. He flipped her around and the next thing she knew, she was sprawled on the grass between Carter's legs, his cock an inch from her mouth and Simon was behind her, lifting her ass.

She grabbed onto Carter's thick member and wrapped her mouth around it, then glided downward, letting it fill her. As he groaned, Simon, who was crouching behind her, pushed his hard cock over her slickness. He glided over her as she suckled Carter's cockhead. She squeezed her thighs around Simon's erection. Oh, God, she was so close that . . .

Simon glided faster and she squeaked around Carter's cock, then pulled him out and moaned as she felt the orgasm begin just from the feel of Simon's cock gliding over her intimate flesh. But then Simon pulled his cock from her so she was squeezing nothingness.

Her body trembled at the intense need, the orgasm fading barely before it had begun.

"Oh, no. Please."

"What is it, ma'am?" Simon asked. "Is there something you need?"

"Oh, yes, please," she whimpered. "I need you inside me. Please, sir. Fuck me."

At her words, Simon growled deep in his throat, then his cock pushed between her legs and—

"Oh, God, yes!!!" she wailed as his cock pushed deep inside her.

Simon pumped into her in deep strokes and her orgasm blossomed again. Her head rested against Carter's groin. Her lips played around the base of his cock as he pumped it with his hand.

Pleasure swamped her senses, filling every cell in her body as she moaned loud and long. Simon groaned and thrust deeper, then shuddered against her, his arms around her waist holding her close to his body.

Her vision was still filled with flashing stars as Simon kissed her back and then drew his long cock from her body, sending quivers through her as it traveled down her passage.

She gazed up at Carter, still needing more. She pushed herself up, then prowled onto his lap. She wrapped her hand around his thick cock and pressed it to her slick, dripping opening and glided down on him.

"Damn, ma'am." Carter grinned, his eyes twinkling. "I'm loving your thank-you."

She smiled, then cupped his cheeks and kissed him. His lips were firm yet tender, moving on hers as he wrapped his arms around her and held her close.

She pushed herself up and down on her knees, taking his cock deep inside her body again and again. Then she squeezed him inside her, to his groan of approval.

"Fuck, baby. You are so sexy."

He wrapped his hands around her hips and guided her up and down faster, then one hand slid between their stomachs and he found her clit.

"Oh, God!" She arched against him, her body trembling with need.

He pivoted his hips upward, filling her faster and deeper as his fingers teased her sensitive bud. Blissful sensations fluttered through her, then exploded inside her, rocking her off the edge of sanity straight to ecstasy.

She moaned in his ear, probably deafening him, but he

kept rocking. Filling her with that wonderful, thick column. She squeezed it, still riding the wave of euphoria.

Then he thrust deep and held her tight to him. She felt his cock quiver, then erupt inside her, driving her orgasm even higher.

Finally, she fell against his chest and sucked in air, breathing in his musky male scent.

"My God, that was sensational," she panted.

Carter chuckled and Simon swept her into his arms and carried her into the house, then up the stairs.

"Now what are you saving me from?" she asked.

"Your breathing seems elevated, ma'am," Carter answered, "so we want to keep an eye on you. We think what you need right now is some bed rest."

"And since you got so wet," Simon added, "we're going to ensure you're nice and warm."

Carter pulled aside the duvet and Simon set her down, then both men crawled into bed with her and held her close between their bodies. She drifted off to sleep in the warmth of their embrace.

After they finished lunch, Rikki glanced at the text that came in on her phone.

"I have a friend who'll be arriving in town from Ashton tomorrow. We're going to get together during the day," she told Carter and Simon.

Carter's eyebrow quirked up. "So you'd rather see this friend than us?"

Her gaze darted to him and he laughed.

"It's okay," Carter said. "We have some errands to do

and some work around the yard. That beautiful garden doesn't stay weeded by itself."

"We can pick you up on the way to shift the next day," Simon said.

"That would be great. But does that mean you're trying to get rid of me?"

"No way." Carter pulled her onto his lap. He squeezed her butt as he pulled her close to his body and kissed her. "You're staying for dinner, then overnight. Right?"

She grinned. "Whatever you say."

The next morning, Rikki asked Tina if she could ride to work with her. She was meeting Tony at the park along the shore of the lake, which was a block from the store where Tina worked. Rikki walked along the sidewalk, the light breeze ruffling the skirt of her sundress. It was a beautiful, hot summer's day.

Rikki settled on the bench near the fountain and waited for Tony to arrive.

She was a little nervous to see him again. He and Jesse had been good friends and the three of them had often been out together. In fact, she'd been very attracted to Tony. If she'd never met Jesse, then she'd often thought there could have been something between her and Tony.

"Well, there's the most beautiful girl in the world."

She glanced up to see Tony walking toward the bench. She almost didn't recognize him since he'd shaved off his scruff. He wore his hair differently, too. The thick, dark mass of waves was gone. Trimmed tight to his scalp. The loss of the scruff made him look younger, but the short cropped hair made him look more rugged and masculine.

"Tony." She stood up and walked toward him. "It's good to see you."

He smiled as he took her hands and glanced up and down at her.

"You look lovely. That's a nice dress."

"Thank you." She'd thought he was going to pull her in for a hug and her heart pounded. There was still an attraction between them and she didn't know how to handle that.

But she was being crazy. He was just an old friend of Jesse's looking her up on the way through town. He and Jesse had been close so of course he'd want to ensure she was okay.

He led her to the bench and they sat down.

"Muldone seems like a nice place. It must be nice having a mountain view."

"It is pretty here," she said. "And I love coming to this park by the lake. I thought we might go canoeing. There's a rental place about a five minute walk from here."

"Sure. Let's do it. Then I'll take you to lunch."

"Well, there's Lakeview Café, which some friends here recommended. Apparently, the food is great and as the name implies, it has a great view of the lake."

"Okay, we have a plan. Lead on."

They walked along the path that followed the shore. Couples and families sat on benches or at the scattered picnic tables around the park while kids raced around playing. Rikki and Tony arrived at the canoe rental place and were soon gliding through the calm water, the sun shining down on them. Rikki was in the front and Tony sat in the back to steer.

Tony updated her on the men at the firehouse. A couple had moved on, but most were still there.

"How are Jim and Roy?" she asked.

Jim Mahoney had been Jesse's mentor. He was an old friend of Jesse's father and had taken Jesse under his wing. Roy Andrews and Jesse had gone through training together and Roy, Tony, and Jesse had been inseparable.

"Jim retired last year. He and his wife have been doing a lot of traveling. Roy's good. He's a lieutenant now." Tony dragged his paddle in the water to turn them to avoid an oncoming canoe. "He's a good leader."

"That's good to hear. I guess he's more serious than he used to be. He used to pull practical jokes all the time. I think he pushed Chief Rogers' patience to the edge more than once."

"Yeah, he got more serious after we lost Jesse. It was tough going with him for a while. He didn't really know how to handle it. But then he buckled down and threw himself into the career, taking courses and pushing himself."

She drew in a deep breath at the sense of loss she felt at the reminder of Jesse's death. But these men had suffered, too. They'd lost a friend . . . a brother.

"I hope he still finds time to laugh," she said, hating to think that his lighthearted spirit had been crushed.

"He has a lot of reasons to laugh these days. He's married and they've just had their first baby. He seems to always have a grin on his face."

She smiled. "That's great."

They continued chatting about common friends until, finally, their hour was up and they paddled to shore.

He pulled the canoe onto the beach and offered his hand to help her out. When she wrapped her fingers around his, a jolt of awareness shot through her. Suddenly, this felt more like a date than a meeting of two old friends. Guilt swelled through her. If Carter and Simon were to see them now, they wouldn't be happy.

"Are you sure this is a good idea?" Carter asked as he got out of the car, then followed Simon toward the park.

"Why not? We're in the area."

It was true; they'd been at the garden center nearby.

"What's the harm in dropping by the restaurant, maybe buying Rikki and her friend a drink," Simon continued. "It's not like we're going to tell her friend that the three of us are involved. We're just two of the firefighters she's working with."

"So you're suggesting we just drop by their table and introduce ourselves."

"Sure, then we'll pick up on Rikki's signals. If she doesn't invite us to join them, then we're on our way." He glanced at Carter. "Aren't you a bit curious to meet one of Rikki's friends? It would be great to hear some of their stories. Find out more about Rikki before we met her."

Carter smiled. "That's true." He scratched his head.

"But I wonder if part of it is that you want to remind Rikki
of what she has here in case being with this old friend makes
Rikki long for back home."

Rikki and Tony walked to the restaurant and sat at a table
on the outside patio overlooking the lovely view.

They ordered and as they enjoyed their meal, he got her
talking about Muldone and her new life here. She told him
about her new roommates, and the work she was doing with
Cassie. She didn't mention anything about doing a calendar or about Simon and Carter.

"So how are you doing?" she asked after the waitress
dropped off their coffees and the check. "It's nice that you're
taking time to visit your parents in Florida."

"Actually, I'm not doing that well."

"Oh?" She gazed at him.

"There was an accident. A fire in one of the old apartment buildings in the east end."

She nodded, gazing at his solemn face.

"Lots of people had already gotten out, but we didn't
know how many people were still inside. When I went in,
the smoke was dense. Could barely see a thing. A couple of
us made our way to the top floor and were working through
the apartments, breaking down doors and going in after sur-
vivors. Most were empty, or the people were already out,
but I went into one place and I heard a small voice crying
out. I found him and his mom in the midst of things. She
had him under her body, trying to protect him from the
flames. I called for help on my radio and Kirk Dempsey got
in there quickly and took the boy out. He was crying for his

mom the whole time, but Kirk hustled him out of there right away." He gazed at her, a haunted look in his eyes. "Good thing, too, because as I started to drag her out, the roof collapsed, then the floor went out. We both fell through, landing on the floor below it. I was knocked out. I was lucky that my brothers got me out of there, but the woman died."

He shook his head. "I know we're supposed to do our best to save people, be happy when we do, and put the rest . . . the ones we couldn't save . . . out of our minds. But sometimes . . ." He shook his head again, his eyes glazing over.

Rikki's heart ached. She reached for his hand.

"Tony, I'm so sorry."

"I regained consciousness as they were loading me into the ambulance. Just in time to see the boy crying as his mother's body was loaded into the one next to me. His eyes . . . the fear and pain in that young face . . . it shook me, you know?"

She squeezed his hand and nodded, though she knew she could never really know what he'd gone through. They sat silently for a few minutes, Rikki unsure what to say.

"Is that why you're going to see your parents?" she asked finally. "To take some time off to work through it?"

"It's more than that, actually. I'm no longer on active duty. The injury I sustained affected my upper spine in such a way that I don't have the necessary strength or mobility in my shoulders and arms to do the job properly. I can still do normal activities, and most jobs won't be affected. I just can't be a firefighter." He shrugged. "Or lift weights."

"Oh, my God. So what are you going to do?" Her heart ached for him. She knew how much he loved the job.

"As you said, I'm going to spend some time with my family. Sort out some things. I know they'd love me to move back south again."

"Is that something you're considering?"

He tilted his head. "I'm considering a lot of things, and Mom is always extolling the benefits of the weather in Florida . . . read that as *no snow* . . . but . . ." He chuckled. "Truth is, I'd miss the snow. I love white Christmases. And going skiing. And tobogganing."

She laughed. "I know what you mean. I've heard they have great tobogganing and skiing here."

He smiled. "Well, maybe no matter where I wind up, I can come and visit you and we'll toboggan together."

She stared at him and saw something in his eyes that sent caution skittering through her. A warmth and . . . more.

She realized she was still holding his hand and she drew back.

"Sure, that would be nice."

He pulled out his wallet, waving away her offer to pay. Once he'd settled up, he walked her outside.

"I have to go now," he said as they walked along the path through the park, "but I'd like you to have dinner with me."

"I'm not sure—"

"You can't say no." He sent her his devilishly charming smile. The one that always got around her defenses. "I'm leaving tomorrow morning and I really want to see you one more time."

Chapter Fifteen

"Okay, sure," Rikki said. "I'd like that."

"Good. How about I drop you off at home, then I can come and pick you up at about six."

"All right. It's a date."

Oh, damn, she wished she hadn't used those words. But surely he wouldn't read anything into it. After all, they were just friends. And they lived in different cities.

He led her to the parking lot just five minutes past the bench where they'd met. He drove her to her house and stopped out front.

"So I'll be back at six. Here, give me your cell and I'll put in my number."

"Okay. I'll see you then."

But before she got out of the car, he took her hand and smiled.

"Rikki, it really is great seeing you again."

She slipped out of the car, disturbed by the warmth in his eyes. Worried that he had more in mind than continuing a friendship.

·   ·   ·

"What the hell was that?" Simon flared. His gut still clenched at the memory of seeing Rikki holding hands with that guy.

He was sitting in the passenger seat as Carter drove home. Carter glanced at him out of the corner of his eye. Simon knew Carter was just as upset, but with his more laid back nature, he handled his emotions about these things better than Simon.

"We don't know why they were holding hands. It could have been any number of reasons."

"Yeah, like he's an old boyfriend here to win her back."

Carter turned onto their street. "Even if that's true, it's not like they had sex. You know Rikki was inexperienced. After all, *you* were the first man she'd ever been with."

"That doesn't mean she won't be tempted. In fact, now that she's had sex, she's more likely to be curious about how it would have been with *him*."

Carter pulled the car into the driveway and Simon marched to the trunk and opened it, then grabbed the big bag of soil and tossed it on the lawn. Carter picked up the grass seed, then went into the garage to grab the rakes so they could get to work.

"It's not like she's going to just walk away from us," Carter said. "Besides the fact I believe she has real feelings for us, she's like a kid with a new toy as far as the adventurous sex goes."

Simon ripped open the bag of soil and started spreading it on the lawn.

"Yeah, but think about it. It's been an uphill battle convincing her it's okay to have a relationship with us given that we're firefighters. And this guy . . . maybe it didn't work out because she wouldn't take the relationship to the next level. Now that she's pushed past her fear . . ." He shrugged.

Carter smiled that infuriatingly smug smile of his.

"Even if she was curious about what it would be like with an old boyfriend, we've got something that guy can't give her."

Simon arched an eyebrow. "And that is?"

Carter chuckled. "There are two of us."

When Rikki answered the door, Tony smiled and glanced at her floral wrap dress in different shades of green and splashes of dark red that set off her auburn hair. She knew it accentuated her waist and showed a little more cleavage than she liked, but he'd said he was taking her to a nice restaurant and this was the dressiest summer outfit she had.

"You look lovely," he said.

"Thank you. You look great, too."

And he did. He wore a charcoal suit and a dove gray shirt with a patterned tie in pewter and soft silver tones. The suit set off his broad shoulders and with his short cropped hair and shadow of whiskers on his face, he seemed an odd mix of gentleman and bad boy.

Once they arrived at the restaurant, which was in one of the hotels in the trendy west end, they sat at a table in an intimate corner. There was a floral centerpiece and a candle casting a soft glow.

"It's a lovely place. I've never been here before."

"I'm told it's the best seafood restaurant in town, and I remember that you used to love shrimp."

"That's true," she said as she unfolded the cloth napkin and placed it on her lap.

The waiter came by and they ordered. The crab cake appetizers arrived quickly and when Rikki tasted them, she sighed at the heavenly flavor.

She glanced at Tony to see him smiling at the euphoric expression on her face.

She straightened in her chair. She felt uncomfortable with him looking at her that way. Indulgently. Clearly happy to see her pleasure.

She sipped her wine.

"Did you spend some time exploring Muldone this afternoon?" she asked.

"No, I spent the afternoon in my hotel room. The pain-killers I take sometimes make me sleepy, so I arrange to have time for a nap when I take them."

"You're still in pain from your injury?"

At her sympathetic expression, he smiled.

"Hey, don't worry about it. I'm sure it'll ease with time, then I'll be back to my old self again."

She couldn't help it. She rested her hand on his. This man had charged into a burning building to save a woman and her child and had been hurt badly enough to change his entire life. He was a hero and he deserved better than fate had dealt him.

"I'm sorry this happened to you. It's just not fair."

He squeezed her hand. "What's done is done. I'm not happy about it, but I have to learn to move forward."

Their gazes locked and there was an intensity between them. He started to speak, but the waiter arrived with their entrees.

As soon as the waiter left, she started telling him how much she enjoyed working with Cassie and even mentioned working with the firefighters on a charity event, though she didn't mention anything about a calendar, not wanting him to think of her taking pictures of half-naked men.

"You just can't tear yourself away from firefighters, can you?" he said with a grin. "I think maybe we're your type." His eyebrow arched. "So are you seeing anyone?"

"Uh . . . no." She didn't know why she'd said it. Probably because she didn't want to answer any questions about who she was seeing and wind up lying because she wouldn't admit to him that she was seeing two men. She still wasn't used to the idea herself.

But she felt guilty. She was in a relationship with Simon and Carter, yet she'd given Tony the idea she was single.

The waiter cleared away their dinner dishes and brought them dessert. Once they were done, Tony paid the bill again, despite her protest, then they walked toward the door and into the lobby. He guided her to the elevator.

"It's only one floor down to the parking garage," she said. "We can walk."

But he pushed the up arrow.

"Actually, when the guys at the firehouse found out I was stopping to see you, they sent something for me to give you, but it was a little too big to bring to the restaurant, so I left it in my room."

"You're staying here?"

"That's right. I thought we'd go up and get it now and maybe you'd stay for an after-dinner drink."

Before she could answer, the door opened and he rested his hand on her lower back and guided her into the elevator. Another couple followed them in.

He pressed number ten and the other man pressed number twelve. The elevator began to move. They rode in silence, then she followed him down the hall. The place had a homey feel, with rich burgundy carpet and wallpaper with a delicate floral design.

"It's a lovely hotel," she said.

He unlocked the door to his room and led her inside.

As soon as she stepped in the door, she saw a large stuffed rabbit sitting on a chair. It had big floppy ears and a pink bow around its neck.

"Oh, my goodness. That's adorable."

Her nickname at the house had been bunny because the first time she'd met them was when Jesse had taken her to their Halloween party and she'd dressed in a fluffy white cat costume that she'd sewn herself, but she'd made the ears a little too long and they'd all teased her that she looked more like a bunny. The name had just stuck after that.

She walked to the chair and picked it up, then hugged it. It was squishy-soft and cuddly. She smiled as she turned to face him, the bunny tight in her arms. Tony walked closer, a warm smile on his face.

"I wish I were that stuffed animal right now." His tone was deep and mellow, and the way he looked at her, with that gleam in his eye, made her stomach tense.

She laughed a little nervously.

"He's very cute. It was very nice of them to send it to me," she said, hoping if she just ignored his comment, he'd stop looking at her like that.

But he stepped closer and took the animal from her arms, then tossed it on the bed. Her eyes widened as he stroked her cheek, his dark brown eyes gazing deeply into her own.

"You know, I've always been attracted to you," he said softly, his warm tone curling around her. "But you were with Jesse and I respected that." He pushed some lose tendrils of hair from her face, his touch soft and tender. "After Jesse died, I started thinking that maybe you and I . . ." He shook his head. "But even after a year, the time never seemed right. Then you went off to college. I realize now that the time never would be right because I felt I'd be betraying Jesse."

He stroked her hair, sending tingles through her. She was mesmerized by the depth of longing in his eyes.

"But when you left Ashton for good"—he shook his head—"I kicked myself. So many years have gone by, and you and I both deserve a chance to be happy."

His arm curled around her waist and he drew her closer. She knew she should pull away, but the familiar musky-spice scent of him and the need in his eyes was compelling. It wasn't lust she saw there, but a longing for a deep connection.

He cupped her face and brought her lips to his. It was so sweet the tender touch nearly broke her heart.

Then he drew back and searched her eyes.

"Tony, I don't know what to say."

"Say that you feel the same way. If you do that, we'll figure something out about how we want to proceed."

He stroked her hair again and the feel of his tender touch played havoc with her senses.

She had actually thought of Tony many times over the years since Jesse's death. She'd missed him. He'd been so much a part of her life when she'd been with Jesse.

But it wasn't just because of his friendship with Jesse. Tony had always been someone she could open up to. He'd always been ready and willing to help when she'd had a problem.

And there was the attraction between them.

She never even considered acting on that, though. Because he was a firefighter, too, and she didn't want to be in that position again.

But Tony was everything she realized she loved in a man: strong, heroic, protective.

And with Tony's injury, he wouldn't be on active duty, so she wouldn't have to deal with the constant fear of losing him.

He smiled, then tightened his arm around her and captured her mouth. His lips moved on hers in a sweet, tender persuasion. His fingers glided under her hair and around her neck, sending tingles along her skin, and he drew her closer still.

As he deepened the kiss she melted against him, wanting what he offered. *Needing* it. Thoughts of going back to Ashton, which was her home, of marrying Tony and living happily ever after . . . Picking up the pieces of her old life . . .

Of finding what she'd lost.

She jerked back.

She flattened her hands on his chest, as much to give herself support as to put some much needed distance between them.

He eased back a little.

"Look," Tony said, "I know this is a lot to take in, and I'm not expecting an answer from you today. I have a lot to deal with right now with getting my life in order. I just wanted to talk to you about this to give you time to think about it. In a couple of weeks, when I head back to Ohio, we can talk again and explore the possibility."

As she stared at him, seeing the hope in his eyes, she couldn't find any words.

After he dropped her off at home and she lay in bed, she hated herself.

God, she'd let Tony kiss her . . . she'd melted into his arms . . . without even a thought about Simon and Carter. What did that say about her feelings for them?

But she knew what it meant. She was still living in fear. She was attracted to Tony, she always had been, but she was in love with Simon and Carter.

Her heart ached.

Yes, it was love. And that terrified her.

In the morning, when Rikki woke up, after a long night of tossing and turning, she checked her phone for messages and found a text from Cassie.

Simon and Carter told me they can't pick you up this morning, but I'll be there at eight.

That was an hour later than the guys would have picked
her up. That meant she could grab some more sleep, but as
tired as she was, she knew she wouldn't get back to sleep
now.

She showered and changed, then put on some coffee and
texted Cassie.

I can just grab the bus.

She grabbed a yoghurt from the fridge, then poured a
cup of coffee and sat down.

*No need. I want to talk to the chief about launching the
calendar. See you soon.*

Rikki sat back and enjoyed the quiet of the morning.
Her roommates were all still sleeping and she could hear
the birds twittering in the trees out back. It was going to
be a beautiful day. The sky was a rich blue, with only a few
fluffy clouds in sight.

She saw Cassie's car pull up in front of the townhouse
and hurried to the door.

"Morning," Rikki said as she slid into the front passenger seat. "Thanks for the ride."

"No problem." Cassie started to drive and Rikki settled into the seat.

"So is everything okay between you and Simon and
Carter?" Cassie asked, giving her a quick sideways glance.

"Sure. Why do you ask?"

"Well, for one, you're in my car, not theirs. I would have assumed you'd have stayed over with them last night."

"I saw a friend from Ashton yesterday who's passing through town."

"A *male* friend?"

"Yeah. So?"

"Do Carter and Simon know you were out with another man?"

"No, it's not like that. He was a friend of Jesse's. And I told them I was seeing a friend. They even suggested a restaurant where I should take him."

"Rikki, is it possible they didn't know it was a man you were seeing?"

"Well, yes, that's probably the case." She stared at her hands. "I didn't make a point of telling them."

"Well, hon, I think maybe they found out. And that they're not too happy about it."

When Rikki and Cassie arrived at the firehouse, Simon and Carter were running the men through drills. Cassie went off to meet with Chief Anderson, and Rikki sat down at the desk in the living area and opened her laptop. She began working on graphics to include in the Web site, since she knew Cassie was proposing the idea to the chief.

Rikki couldn't take more shots for the calendar while all the men were busy.

The alarm sounded around midmorning and the men all ran to the trucks and took off. It was early afternoon when they returned. Cassie and Rikki had made up some hearty sandwiches for lunch and when the men filed back in, they hurrahed in approval.

But Simon and Carter shed their gear and went straight into a meeting with the chief.

A few minutes later, Dodge walked up to her.

"Hey, we're available for pictures now, if you're ready. You can start with me."

She remembered the last photo shoot with Dodge, where he was in the bed looking almost naked and oh, so sexy, sending her heart fluttering.

She hadn't gotten calendar shots of him yet, so this worked out well.

"That's great. Thanks," Rikki said.

Cassie smiled as Dodge headed to the truck. "I'm glad I'm here for this photo shoot," Cassie said. "Seeing Dodge with his shirt off and all those lovely tattoos." Cassie sighed, beaming as she stood up and followed Rikki outside.

Rikki took pictures for a couple of hours. Luckily, the weather cooperated, with only a few puffy clouds hampering the bright sunshine periodically.

Once they were done, Rikki and Cassie sat down at the laptop to review the new photos.

When Rikki saw Simon and Carter walk into the room, she stood up and headed them off.

"Hi. You seem to be having a busy day," she observed, trying to start a conversation.

"Yeah, and it still is," Simon said curtly as he headed for the door. "We've got to do an inspection of the equipment right now."

She followed them out to the truck. "You don't have time for a coffee first?"

"Afraid not," Simon said.

They walked along the side of the truck and opened one of the compartments, revealing oxygen tanks and other equipment.

She watched them start going through the equipment, knowing she should leave them to their work, but her stomach was tied up in knots and she had to say something.

"I get the feeling you're avoiding me," she blurted.

"Rikki, we're just busy today," Carter said.

She shook her head. "No, it's more than that. I can sense it. Tell me what's wrong."

"The whole point is," Simon said, "we don't want to talk about it here. It would be more appropriate where there aren't other people around."

"Talk about what?" she persisted.

Anger flared in Simon's blue eyes, but then it flickered to indifference.

Carter glanced at Simon, then to Rikki.

"We saw you with a man yesterday," Carter said. "In a restaurant. And you two looked pretty cozy."

She frowned. "What do you mean 'cozy'?"

"It means," Simon flared, "you were holding his hand. And looking at him in *that way*."

"I don't know what way you mean, but he's just a friend."

"A *male* friend that you've known for quite a while. Possibly dated?" Simon demanded.

"I never dated him," she said. "He's a firefighter . . . he was one of Jesse's friends . . . and he was telling me about an accident on the job. Something that affected him emotionally and physically."

"That's rough," Carter said sympathetically.

Simon turned his assessing gaze toward her.

"And why did you go up to his room after dinner?"

Guilt washed through her, even as she wondered how he knew that. Of course, someone who knew Simon or Carter could easily have spotted her getting on the elevator with Tony . . . going up.

"He had a gift for me from Jesse's firehouse."

Carter's warm eyes gazed at her. She could tell he saw her pain.

"If you tell us nothing happened in the room," Carter said, "we'll believe you."

Between Simon's cool blue gaze and Carter's amber querying one, she felt her heart sink.

"Nothing happened the way you mean, but . . ." She drew in a breath. She didn't feel right hiding it from them. "He did kiss me."

Simon's gaze cut through her like razor blades. "And did you kiss him back?"

Chapter Sixteen

Rikki's chest tightened.

At her hesitation, anger . . . and pain . . . flared in Simon's eyes.

"Simon, please. I—"

But the alarm blared, then the door opened and the other firefighters hurried toward the truck.

"We can talk about this later," Simon said coolly. "But not until after shift. I think you should go home when Cassie leaves."

"Did I totally blow it?" Rikki asked as Cassie drove her home.

"I don't know, but maybe it's for the best. This Tony sounds perfect for you. You said you've been attracted to him for a long time. And he's got the heart of a firefighter, with all those wonderful heroic characteristics, but he won't actually be going out to fight fires, so you won't have the painful, worry-filled nights. I mean, don't get me wrong, I hate the fact that if you choose him, it means you'll probably move back to Ashton, or maybe even Florida, so I won't get to see you much." She rested her hand on Rikki's arm. "But, honey, I want you to be happy."

"What if my happiness is with Simon and Carter, but they won't want me back now?"

"I love Simon and Carter, and I love you, but from everything you've ever told me, being with any active firefighter will *not* make you happy. It'll just leave you an emotional wreck."

Rikki sighed as Cassie pulled up to her townhouse.

"Are you sure you don't want to go out to dinner with me? Then grab some drinks?" Cassie asked.

"No. I don't really feel up to it. I'm just going to tune into Netflix and veg."

"And feel sorry for yourself."

Rikki forced a grin. "Well, if I don't, who will?"

Cassie laughed. "Not me. You've got three sexy firemen mooning over you, two of which you've been having hot, kinky sex with. And I'm sure you've got your choice of any of the others at the firehouse." She grinned. "I've seen how Dodge and some of the others look at you."

Rikki got out of the car. "Just what I need. More men's hearts to break." She gazed at her friend. "See you, Cassie." Then she closed the car door and went inside.

Rikki walked to the couch carrying the vanilla pudding she'd just made, hot off the stove, and sat in front of the television again in her pajamas. The can of soup she'd heated for dinner two hours ago, followed by the half bag of chips she'd munched, just hadn't hit the spot.

She set the huge bowl of pudding on her lap and flicked on the next episode of the sitcom that Anna had recommended to her, then started eating the creamy comfort food as she lost herself in the show again.

Anna and Mel had come in while she was having dinner—Anna's car was in the shop so Mel had been driving her to and from work the last few days—but they both had dinner dates and disappeared out the door again. Tina had probably gone straight out after work.

Why couldn't she be as free and easy as her roommates? Just enjoy a lighthearted connection with someone. Share some laughs. Casual sex. And no heartbreak.

It was after ten when she heard the front door open and Tina come in. She was talking to someone and the other voice was male. They stepped from the entrance and Tina smiled.

"Hey, you're not off with a sexy fireman tonight?" Tina asked.

"No, just spending a quiet night at home."

Tina eyed the bowl on her lap. "Yeah, I can see that." She turned to her date, who looked vaguely familiar. "Why don't you go upstairs? I'll see you there in a few minutes."

He smiled. "Sure thing." He glanced at Rikki. "Nice to see you again."

Once he was gone, Tina sat down beside Rikki and picked up the bag of chips and ate a few while she watched the television.

"Is this season two?" Tina asked.

"No, still season one."

"Oh, so you haven't gotten to the part where Cynthia dies."

Rikki's eyes widened and she stared at Tina in horror. "Why did you—?"

But Tina broke out in giggles. "You didn't really think I'd give you a spoiler like that, did you?"

Rikki frowned. "You better not have."

She grabbed a handful of chips from the bag Tina was holding.

"Where have I seen your date before?" Rikki asked.

"That's Len. He was the one who was going to ask you to dance at Rango's but you diverted him my way with your freeze-out." She popped another chip in her mouth. "Thanks again for that."

"Anytime." Rikki ate another spoonful of pudding.

"So I've got to ask. Why are you sitting here all alone, pigging out on junk food? Something go wrong between you and your guys? Which one are you with, anyway?"

Rikki sighed. "Your date's waiting for you. You don't want to hear about this now."

Tina settled back into the couch and grabbed a handful of chips from the bag.

"Don't worry about that. It won't hurt him to wait a bit." She grinned. "In fact, it'll make it all the hotter because of the anticipation."

"Or he'll fall asleep," Rikki teased.

Tina laughed. "Either way, I know I'll be able to get a rise out of him quick enough. Now tell me what's going on."

Rikki explained her issue with having a relationship

with a firefighter and how she'd pushed past the superficial level to start a sexual fling with Simon and Carter.

"Wait," Tina said. "You're saying you'd never been with a man before *at all*?"

"That's right."

"So your first time—ever—was a threesome?"

Rikki nodded. Tina's face broke out in a huge smile.

"Well, way to go, baby!" She munched a couple of chips. "But now you're falling for them, right?" She nudged Rikki with her shoulder. "Don't even try to deny it. I've seen it in your eyes since day one. The way you look at them—and them at you—it's clear as day."

"I do have feelings for them, but I don't know what to do about that. If I go into a long-term relationship with them—whatever that even means with three of us—I'll still be a mess worrying about them getting hurt."

Tina shrugged. "People get hurt all the time, no matter what job they do. Someone you love could get hurt in a car accident, a plane crash. He could drown, fall in the shower, trip down the stairs."

Rikki's jaw dropped as she stared at Tina. "Well, aren't you just a lovely ray of sunshine?"

Tina laughed. "Just calling it like it is. And you"—she grinned—"you at least have a spare."

"Tina, you're awful."

"I'm just saying that—"

"I know. I get it. I really do. They asked me to give the relationship a chance, and I said I would."

"Good for you."

Rikki sighed. "Then I messed up."

She told her about Tony coming to town, and how she went up to his room. And kissed him.

"Simon and Carter found out about it and now . . ." Rikki shrugged.

"So do you feel the same way about this guy that you do for Simon and Carter?"

"It's different. He's got all the same attractive characteristics. I mean, clearly there's something about firefighters—they're heroic, responsible, protective—that I'm attracted to. Tony has all that without the danger of the job."

"Well, I guess you just have to ask yourself, do you want to settle for *safe* or for *love?*"

Tina finished watching the last five minutes of the sitcom episode with Rikki, then went upstairs, where she had a man waiting for her.

Unlike Rikki, with just an empty bed to welcome her.

After two more episodes, Rikki finally turned off the TV and headed to her room. As she went up the stairs, she heard a door open and close. By the time she got to the top floor, Tina opened the bathroom door and entered the hallway.

"Good night," Tina said as she slipped back into her room.

Rikki went into her own room and climbed into bed, then lay staring at the ceiling. She heard voices coming up the stairs a little later. She was pretty sure it was Anna and her date.

As Rikki lay in the darkness, she soon heard soft moans through the wall. Tina and her date starting another round.

Probably the same thing was going on in Anna's room one floor down, too.

All Rikki could think about was how she wanted to be in bed with Simon and Carter right now. The three of them sharing intimate, loving touches. Pleasing each other. Making each other come.

Then lying in one another's arms and just sharing the intimacy of the love they shared.

Her heart clenched. Because she did love them. And she was pretty sure they loved her.

She ached inside at her stupid screwup that had caused her two men pain.

She knew she had to convince them that she would embrace this relationship and give it every chance to work. Somehow she would find a way to get past her fear.

Simon stared at the ceiling from his bed. He should grab some sleep while the place was quiet, but his brain kept swirling around the conversation earlier with Rikki.

His gut clenched at the thought of her kissing another man. The guy making a play for her—he could understand that. But the fact that Rikki had kissed him back. Pain lanced through him. That meant she had feelings for the guy.

That meant they could lose her.

The alarm went off and he pushed back the covers and dodged to his feet. He grabbed his pants and pulled them on and hurried out the door. Carter was ahead of him.

"Did you hear the address?" Carter said as they climbed inside the truck and sat down.

"Five thirty-five Ramsey," Dodge said.

Simon's gut clenched. "That's right beside Rikki's."

The truck raced through the streets, sirens and lights blazing. Her place was part of a five-unit row house. Simon's heart pounded as they sped there, hoping to hell she was okay. He could see the same concern in Carter's eyes. The other men's, too. They all thought the world of Rikki.

And, fuck, Simon couldn't stop thinking about the way he and Carter had left things with her.

His gut clenched. If she got hurt in this fire, how could he ever forgive himself?

As soon as they got there, they jumped out of the truck and he and Carter started barking orders to their men. The middle unit of the row house was five thirty-five where the fire had clearly started, but just as he'd feared, the fire had spread to the two units on either side of it. The left one was where Rikki lived.

Chief Anderson's vehicle pulled up and he raced toward Simon. Several of the men, on Carter's orders, had stormed into the three blazing units to look for anyone trapped inside, most going into the middle unit, since it was in the worst state. Simon was happy to see he sent Dodge and Tanner into the left unit. All their men were good, but he knew that if Rikki were trapped, Dodge's strength and Tanner attention to detail would go a long way.

As Simon gave the chief an update, one of the men inside radioed that there was someone pinned under some fallen debris in the right unit, so the chief ordered Carter to go in and help.

"I'm going into the leftmost unit, Chief," Simon said.

"Hurry," he said as he stared at the burning building, assessing. "From the look of things, we don't have much time."

Simon raced toward Rikki's unit, but when he saw Anna, Rikki's roommate, at the ambulance being given oxygen, he hurried to her.

"Anna, is everyone out of your place?"

She looked up at him in a daze. She was holding the hand of a man sitting beside her, also with an oxygen mask on.

"I'm Simon. Rikki's friend."

She clutched his sleeve. "The smoke detectors went off right away and woke us up, but the place filled with smoke in minutes." She shook her head. "It happened so fast."

His heart pounded. "So Rikki and the others got out okay?"

Her eyes filled with anxiety and she pulled the mask down and spoke in short gasps. "I . . . don't know. The house was quiet when I got home. I don't know who was there. I got a text out to Tina as I ran down the stairs, but then the smoke was too thick." She shook her head, her fingers tightening around her boyfriend's sleeve. "There were flames in the living room. I dropped my phone and just kept running."

He squeezed her shoulder, giving her a reassuring smile, then lurched toward the house. His fellow firefighters were bringing people out of the middle unit and leading them to waiting ambulances. He heard someone call out that it was all clear.

Someone tugged at his sleeve as he ran and he spun around, praying to God it was Rikki. But he came face-to-face with Tina.

"Simon?" Tina asked.

"Tina, do you know if Rikki is still in the house?"

"I don't know, but I think so. I saw her go into bed. Len and I went out for ice cream after that and then I got a text from Anna telling me the place was on fire. I texted Rikki and Mel right away. Mel's okay, but . . ." She stared at him with wide eyes. "I haven't heard anything back from Rikki."

He glanced up at the window he knew was Rikki's. Flames were blazing from the room.

As he raced toward the door, pulling on his mask, black smoke started billowing from the units. Fuck, that was bad news. He rushed inside.

It was dark with smoke. He could barely see.

"Couldn't find anyone in the house, Lieutenant," Tanner said as he hurried into sight.

Dodge was right behind him.

Simon kept moving to where he knew the stairs were. "I think Rikki's on the third floor."

The two men turned to follow, but the chief's voice sounded on the radio.

"Get the hell out of there, everyone. Now!"

Simon ignored the call and raced up the stairs. The weight of the equipment slowed him down from how fast he could normally take stairs, but he knew he was making record time.

The thought kept spiking through his brain.

He had to save Rikki.

Carter raced out of the unit two over from Rikki's. The chief had ordered them out. They'd gotten the woman free just in time and he helped carry her out on a stretcher.

But the whole time his mind was on Rikki. Was she out?

He glanced at the building. The bright flames towered into the night sky, smoke billowing up into the darkness. Bits of flaming debris were falling from the building.

The blaze was still out of control.

He knew Simon would move heaven and earth to find her and get her to safety, just as he would.

He helped get the woman inside the ambulance, then glanced around at the turmoil around him. He spotted Tina and headed toward her. She stood with the man he'd seen her dancing with the night they'd first met Rikki.

He raced over to her. "Tina! Where's Rikki?"

"I don't know." She looked close to tears. "We think she's still inside. Simon went in after her and he hasn't come out yet."

"What?"

He stared up at the building. It was bad. Many of the windows had shattered as the frames began to buckle. The chief had already called everyone out, which meant not only Rikki was in danger, but also Simon.

"Davies, get the hell out of there!" the chief bellowed into the radio.

"I'm sure Rikki's up here, Chief," Simon's voice sounded in the radio, "but I can't find her."

A loud groan sounded in Carter's earpiece, then what he was sure was falling debris. The radio went dead.

"Oh, my God." Tina covered her mouth as she stared at the roof.

Chapter Seventeen

Carter followed her gaze to see part of the roof had collapsed. His heart pounded. God, had he just lost both Rikki and Simon? He turned to Chief Anderson. "Chief, we've got to go in and get him."

"No way. I'm not chancing anyone else's life. That building is about to come down."

"Tina!" a familiar voice called out.

He turned toward the sound, a prickle running up his spine.

He sucked in a breath as he saw Rikki, being held back by one of the police officers trying to keep bystanders away from the scene.

"Rikki!" He raced toward her.

When the police officer saw Carter in his gear approaching, he let her through.

"Carter!" She threw herself into his arms.

He hugged her tight, relief flooding through him that she was alive.

"I'm sorry, I didn't recognize you," she panted. "I saw Tina and I was so glad she's okay."

She pulled back. "Are the others okay? Did everyone get out?"

"Fuck, Rikki. We thought you were inside." He grabbed her hand and dragged her along with him.

"Chief, Lieutenant Davies is in there looking for Rikki and she's right here."

Rikki's hand tightened around his. "Simon's in there?"

She stared up at the burning building, the sagging structure a sure sign of the imminent structural collapse.

"Oh, my God," Rikki said, her hands covering her mouth.

"Davies," Chief said into the radio, "if you can hear me, Rikki is safe and sound out here." Then his voice boomed. "So get your ass out of there!"

Carter couldn't stand it any longer. He dragged Rikki with him to Tina and pressed her to her friend, then raced toward the building.

Rikki clung to Tina's hand, staring at the blazing building in front of them. The acrid smell of smoke filled her lungs. Flames swelled outward and up from the top floors, like a torrential flood of bright orange water gushing into the sky. It was terrifying.

And Simon was in there.

"Oh, God, this is a nightmare."

Tina squeezed her hand. "Rikki, I'm sure everything's going to be okay."

"How can it be okay? Simon's in there right now, probably hurt, or dead. And now Carter is . . ." But a sob closed up her throat, killing the words.

"Damn it, what the hell are you doing, Fenn?" the chief called out.

"Just let me check the main floor, Chief," Carter answered.

"I said no. That's an order!"

Carter hesitated at the door, peering back at the chief.

Thank God he didn't barrel inside. Rikki desperately wanted Simon to be okay, but she didn't want Carter in harm's way, too.

"Wait, Chief. I can hear his personal alarm. He's down, but he's close."

"Fuck!" the chief exclaimed. "You've got thirty seconds."

"I'm going in, too, Chief." Dodge stared at his commanding officer, waiting for the okay.

The chief nodded.

Rikki watched the two of them pull on their oxygen masks as they raced inside. Her heart pounded in her chest, counting off the seconds these brave men were inside that horrific deathtrap.

Time stood still, torturing her with all the possibilities.

Tina slid her arm around her waist.

"He'll be okay. I just know he'll be okay," Tina said like a mantra.

The black smoke thickened and the building creaked. Rikki held her breath.

Then . . .

"Look!"

Tina pointed toward the door, and through the haze,

Rikki could see movement. Shapes coming out of the building.

Two men.

"Oh, God, no." Her heart crumpled.

But then she realized there was a third man between them. The two were supporting him, his head leaning forward.

As they stepped out of the worst of the smoke, she could see it was Simon being propped up between Carter and Dodge. He was limping.

Someone raced up with a wheeled stretcher and helped him onto it, then rushed him to a nearby ambulance. She raced after it, but Carter headed her off.

"You've got to give it a minute," Carter said.

"What's wrong? Is he okay?"

"His oxygen tank ran out and he took in a lot of smoke."

For the first time, she realized Carter didn't have his mask. He must have given it to Simon when he found him inside.

"He got hit by some falling debris, so he has some cuts and bruises, but he should be okay."

She didn't know what Carter wasn't telling her. She hoped he wasn't just trying to calm her down with an overly optimistic assessment. Or an outright lie.

"Can I go to the hospital with him?"

"I'll drive you," Tina offered.

Carter nodded. "That's a good idea. I'll meet you over there as soon as I can."

Then he wrapped his big arms around her and held her

close. He stroked her hair back and his lips brushed her temple.

"Don't worry, baby. He'll be okay."

As soon as they got to the hospital, Rikki rushed into the building, Tina right behind her, and they hurried to Emergency. But no one would tell them anything, no matter how much she pleaded.

About twenty minutes later, Carter arrived. He strolled right to Rikki, dropped the backpack he was carrying, and gave her a warm hug.

"They won't tell us how Simon's doing," she said, her eyes wide and her stomach roiling.

"It's okay," he said in a soothing voice. "I'll go find out."

He walked across the waiting room to the reception desk. The two uniformed woman there greeted him warmly and he chatted with them for a few minutes, then handed them the backpack.

He walked back to Rikki and sat down. She wrapped her hand around his as she gazed up at him, her stomach clenched. He squeezed gently.

"He's doing fine. He took in a lot of smoke, so they put him on oxygen and they're watching him for a while. He also has a gash on his leg and some burns, but they're not too severe. They're patching him up."

His words eased her anxiety a bit, but the idea that Simon had been burned upset her.

"When can we see him?" she asked.

"Probably not for an hour or so, but then we can take him home."

"Really?"

Carter smiled. "Really. I brought a change of clothes for him because I figured as much."

"Do you know what caused the fire?" Tina asked.

"The investigator's still checking it out," Carter said, "but it looks like an electrical fire in the unit next door."

He turned back to Rikki and stroked her hair behind her ear. His tender touch sent warmth through her.

"And in case you're wondering, you'll stay with us. Right?"

She let a small smile creep across her face. "Thank you. I would love that."

He hugged her and she melted against him, loving the feel of his protective arms around her.

When she finally drew back, Carter turned to Tina.

"Do you have somewhere to stay? Because if you don't, we have a guest room."

Tina smiled brightly. "That would be great. Really. But I have a sister in town. She'd kill me if I didn't stay with her." She shrugged. "Besides, she and I are the same size, so I can bum clothes from her. An important consideration since this is all I've got right now."

She gestured to the worn jeans and T-shirt she'd pulled on to go to the ice cream place that stayed open twenty-four hours during tourist season.

Tina glanced at her watch. "In fact, I should head over

there now. I texted her a while ago to let her know I was all right and I know she's anxious to see me."

She stood up and gave Rikki a hug. "Keep in touch, okay?"

Rikki nodded. "Thanks for staying with me."

Tina patted her hand. "Of course."

The next hour seemed to take forever to pass, but eventually a nurse rolled Simon out in a wheelchair.

As soon as she saw him, Rikki bolted to her feet and lurched toward him.

"Simon." She stopped in front of him and hesitated, not sure if she should touch him or not. She didn't want to hurt him.

He smiled and opened his arms and she leaned in and hugged him. His big arms closed around her, feeling as strong as ever.

"I was so worried," she murmured against his ear, feeling tears prickle at her eyes.

"Believe me, I know exactly how you felt. I thought you were trapped in that blaze."

She leaned back and saw the intensity of emotions in his eyes, showing just how desperately he'd been worried about her.

"Hey, you two. Let's roll." Carter grasped the handles of the wheelchair.

Rikki straightened up and followed Carter to the exit as he pushed Simon in the chair.

"Wait here while I pull the car up." Carter disappeared out the glass door.

She turned back to Simon. He looked pale.

"Are you in pain?" she asked.

"Not right now. They gave me some painkillers. But ask me in a couple of hours."

Carter was back in a flash and soon they were all in the car. When they got back to the house, she helped Carter guide Simon up the stairs to his room. The painkillers they'd given him were pretty strong and he was a bit wobbly.

Simon stripped down to his boxers and climbed into the bed. Rikki was disturbed by the large bandage around his right thigh and another on the left side of his torso. She hesitated, then kissed his cheek.

"I'll see you when you wake up," she said.

But before she could move away, he grabbed her hand and tugged her back.

"Where do you think you're going? I want you right here."

"But you're hurt."

He smiled. "All the more reason for some comfort."

She smiled, too, and dropped her jeans to the floor, then she slid in beside him on the right side. He wrapped his arm around her and drew her close. She tried not to brush against the bandage on his leg, but he pulled her closer and her leg rested lightly against his.

"Now I can get some sleep," he murmured as he closed his eyes.

His deep sigh of contentment relaxed her and she realized she was pretty sleepy. Soon she drifted off right alongside him.

Simon woke up feeling like he'd been hit by a truck. He shifted and the pain in his leg and torso jolted through him.

"Are you okay?"

He glanced toward Rikki's voice to see her lying beside him, her green eyes wide.

"Yeah, just a little stiff," he lied.

She bit her lip and stared at the bandage on his torso. She ran her fingers along the edges of it, her soft touch triggering a longing deep inside him. The last time they'd talked, she'd told him she'd kissed another man, and he'd been struggling with the pain of that revelation ever since.

He didn't want to lose her.

"Can I get you something?" she asked. "Coffee? I could bring you breakfast in bed."

He smiled. "Not if it means you leaving the bed." He slid his arm around her and drew her close. She snuggled up to his side, resting her hand on his chest, avoiding the bandages.

A tap sounded at the bedroom door.

"Come in," Simon called.

The door opened and Carter stood in the doorway.

"I thought I heard voices in here. I've got bacon cooked and pancakes ready to put on the griddle."

"And I smell coffee," Simon said. "Sounds great."

Rikki hopped out of the bed and hurried around to his side. All she wore was her T-shirt, leaving her long, beautiful legs bare, and her long auburn hair bounced around her shoulders in glossy waves.

God, she was so sweet and sexy. All he wanted to do was pull her back into bed with him and hold her all day.

But she drew back the covers and held out her hand to help him up. He took it and started to ease up, then jerked her hand toward him, catching her off guard. She fell against him, her eyes widening in horror, but he just laughed as he scooped her into his arms and squeezed, despite the pain. He wrapped his hand around her head and drew her in for a kiss, then swirled his tongue deep into her mouth. When he released her, her breathlessness filled him with a deep sense of satisfaction.

"I really am fine," he murmured against her ear.

Then he sat up. She scrambled to her feet.

"I see you're going to be tricky to take care of," she said.

"And you intend to take care of me?" he asked with eyebrows raised.

She smiled. "Well, I need to earn my keep somehow. Carter invited me to stay here since my townhouse is . . ." Her smile faded. "Gone."

In her eyes, he saw a plethora of emotions. She might not have been in the house when it burned down, but her roommates had been, and they'd been in danger. Also, all her stuff was toast.

And he knew damned well this was going to push her buttons about losing him or Carter on the job. It had brought it home fast and hard for her.

She was here now, caught up in her concern for him, but once things settled down and she really understood that he was fine, would she end it with them for good?

After breakfast, Simon sat on the couch reading while Rikki cleaned up the dishes and Carter did some yard work.

All day, Rikki waited on him hand and foot. She and Carter prepared a nice dinner together then afterward, they all decided to sit down together in the living room to watch a movie.

Rikki sat beside Simon, leaving several inches between them, her back rigid.

"You can come in a little closer," Simon said. "I'm not fragile."

"You're hurt. I don't want to bump anything."

He laughed. "That's funny. Because I'd love it if you'd *bump* some things."

He wrapped his arm around her and snuggled her to his side.

She leaned her head against his shoulder. "You joke, but you were in that burning building because of me. You could have been *killed* because of me."

He stroked her shimmering auburn hair from her face. "Do you really think anything would stop me from moving heaven and earth to save you from danger?"

She chewed her lower lip. "But you could have been killed. I was so worried about you."

His gut clenched at the agony he saw in her eyes. The same agony he'd felt when he'd thought she was in danger. When he thought about her trapped . . . hurt . . . maybe even dead.

He leaned in close, gliding his hand along her cheek and through her hair. "That's exactly how I felt about you."

Fuck, this was the fear she would face every single day if they allowed this relationship to continue. It was the reason she'd tried to avoid getting involved with him and Carter.

Yet they had persisted. Just worried about what they wanted. What *they* thought was best. Not thinking about what it meant for her. The pain it would cause her.

If they really cared about Rikki's best interest—Simon's heart clenched tightly in his chest—then maybe they should let her go.

He stroked her cheek. But how could he when he knew he was falling in love with her?

Chapter Eighteen

Rikki was caught off guard by the intense emotion in Simon's eyes. Love shone so brightly in those blue depths she felt her heart swell in response.

Carter returned from the kitchen with some sodas and a big bowl of popcorn. He set them on the coffee table and stared at the two of them.

"What the hell did I miss?"

Rikki swallowed the lump in her throat. "I was just telling Simon how worried I was about him when he went into the townhouse after me."

She turned to Carter, and took his hand. "You, too, when you went in to get Simon."

Carter knelt down in front of her and squeezed her hand, then pressed it to his lips.

"This is what we do. And when you're the one who needs us, you better believe we're going to do everything in our power to bring you out alive. Do you understand?"

She nodded, blinking back tears. "Yes, I do," she whispered.

Carter leaned in and kissed her, his lips tender on hers. Moving softly. She opened, welcoming his tongue as it dipped inside, then stroked gently. She wrapped her arms around him and held him close as they kissed passionately.

Heat welled through her, coiling through her stomach and outward, making her tremble. Carter ran his hands down her sides, then grasped her hips and arched against her. The bulge that pressed against her was thick and rock-hard.

When their lips parted, Simon cupped her cheek and drew her toward him into a kiss. His lips—firmer and more insistent—moved on hers with passionate intent.

"You know"—the words rumbled from Simon's chest—"I've changed my mind about the movie."

She stared at him wide-eyed, aching for the feel of his and Carter' bodies close to hers. Naked. Their hands stroking her. Their lips caressing.

"But you need to rest," she said breathlessly.

"I've had lots of rest. What I haven't had enough of is you."

"I second that." Carter's lips nuzzled her neck, sending tingles dancing along her spine.

She gazed at his glowing amber eyes then back to Simon uncertainly.

Simon stroked her cheek. "Since you're worried about me, why don't I just relax and . . . watch."

She settled against the back of the couch and stroked her hands over her breasts. Her nipples pushed against her bra, making peaks against the thin fabric of her T-shirt.

"Like this?" she asked.

"Mmm," Simon murmured, his eyes lighting up, "that's a great start."

She laughed and ran her hand over his jeans, feeling his cock swelling under the fabric.

"It's certainly getting my engine running." Carter's hand stroked over his bulge.

"Yeah? Maybe you should show me." Rikki's gaze fell to his swollen ridge.

Carter's face beamed with his wide smile. He unzipped and drew out his long, rigid cock. She stared at it hungrily. She glanced at Simon to see his eyes darkening as she leaned forward, then wrapped her hand around Carter's thick member. She stroked it, then leaned forward and kissed the tip. It was hard and hot against her lips. She opened her mouth and took him inside. Just a little at a time.

"Ah, baby, that feels so good."

She took his whole cockhead in her mouth and licked it thoroughly, to his murmurs of approval. She stroked his shaft with her hand as she began to suckle.

She released him and leaned back again. She pulled her T-shirt over her head and tossed it aside. Then she unzipped her jeans and wriggled them down her hips and kicked them away. Carter watched her raptly, his cock pointing straight forward.

She rested her head against the couch and cupped her breasts, then caressed them.

"Do you like watching me, Simon?" she asked.

His liquid-silk sapphire eyes were locked on her hands.

"Oh, yeah, baby."

She tugged down the lace of her bra to expose one breast, then teased the nipple between her fingers.

"You like me making my nipples hard for you?" She revealed the other breast and teased that nipple to a ripe, swollen bud, too.

He licked his lips, nodding.

She turned to Carter, and saw his amber eyes were ablaze.

She glided her hands down her stomach, watching the two men watching her hungrily. She slid her fingers under her panties and found the soft folds hidden there.

"Ohhh," she moaned softly. "I'm so wet." She ran her fingers through the slickness.

The intensity of their hot gazes sent ripples of delight through her.

Slowly, she drew the front of her panties down, revealing her petals. She held the panties with one hand while she stroked her wet flesh with the other.

Carter leaned forward and captured one of her nipples in his mouth. She moaned softly as his heat surrounded her. His tongue swirled over her—round and round—driving her wild. Then he suckled and she moaned.

His hand glided down her stomach, then his fingers joined hers gliding over her slit. When his finger pushed inside her, she moaned and arched upward against his hand.

He chuckled. "You *are* ready."

He stood up and dropped his jeans to the floor, then his boxers, but before he could kneel down again, she wrapped her hand around his cock and drew it to her mouth again. She wrapped her lips around him and surged forward, swallowing him deep inside.

Simon stroked her hair back and held it in a handful behind her head as she squeezed Carter in her mouth. Carter moaned. She glided back, then forward again. Taking him in and out.

"Yeah, that's right, baby," Simon said. "I love watching you suck Carter's cock." He leaned in close and whispered in her ear, "I love watching you make him come."

Carter's hand wrapped around her head and he urged her to a faster pace. She took him deep. Faster. Squeezing and sucking.

She could feel him tensing. Getting close.

She squeezed his base, and slid her mouth free, then stroked with her hand. She licked his cockhead like a lollipop, lapping her tongue over the entire surface with a delightful thoroughness.

Then she leaned back and slid off her panties, then opened her legs. Carter knelt down and pressed close to her, between her knees. He reached behind her and unfastened her bra then pulled it away.

He leaned forward and suckled her right nipple. She sighed happily, her eyelids falling closed. Then she felt Simon's mouth on her left breast and she sucked in air.

"Oh, that feels so good." Her voice was breathy and filled with need. "Please, Carter. I want you to fuck me."

His mouth moved away, leaving her nipple aching for more. Simon sat back again and watched as Carter pressed his cock to her wet flesh and glided the tip up and down.

The feel of his hot, hard flesh caressing her sent wild surges of delight through her.

"Oh, yes." She sucked in a breath. "I want to feel you inside me. Your big hard cock filling me."

Carter smiled and pushed forward a little, his cockhead stretching her. More and more as he moved slowly into her.

Then he stopped, his cockhead barely halfway in, and she groaned.

He laughed, then drew back and rocked forward again. This time he slid a little deeper, his cockhead not quite all the way in. Then drew back again.

She ached for him. Needing him inside her.

Simon watched Carter's cock teasing her. He freed his own cock and wrapped his hand around it. Rikki bit her lip as she watched Simon's hand glide up and down, wishing Carter would just surge deep inside her.

Carter began to move again. Slowly. Pushing into her.

His cockhead was fully inside her now, and she squeezed around him, not wanting him to pull out again. This time, he didn't. His hard cock pushed deeper still. Stretching her tight passage. Caressing it as he moved farther and farther inside her. She wrapped her arms around him and pulled him closer.

His cock filled her all the way, his shaft a thick pillar of flesh embedded in her softness. She squeezed around it, loving the marble-hard feel of it.

"Oh, God," she said in breathy gasps. "You feel so good inside me."

He pressed his forehead to hers and smiled.

"And it's going to feel so much better in a few seconds."

She sucked in a breath as he drew back, his thick plum-sized cockhead dragging along her passage. She tightened around him, the feel of his withdrawing cock filling her with euphoria.

Then, just as he almost slipped away entirely . . . he thrust forward again.

"Oh, God," she gasped, clinging tightly to him.

Simon stroked her hair back and his lips played along the side of her neck as Carter pulled back, then thrust deep again.

Simon's hand cupped her breast and she rested her hand over his, squeezing him around her. Carter drove into her.

"Do you like Carter's cock inside you?" Simon murmured against her ear.

"Yes. Oh, so much."

Carter thrust again. And again.

Now he was filling her in a steady motion. His thick cock driving into her. Pleasure fluttering through her. Coiling in her belly and spiraling outward.

Simon gently pinched her nipple and she arched against his hand. Carter drove in harder.

"Oh, yes!" Pleasure rippled through her. Quivering over every nerve ending. Building higher and higher.

"Do you want him to fuck you harder?" Simon's breath wisped along her skin, making the hairs on her neck spike upright.

"Yes. Fuck me harder, Carter," she pleaded.

His amber eyes were fierce with need and he plunged into her harder and faster. She gasped, so close she could feel the edge of ecstasy caressing her consciousness. She arched against him, opening wider. Allowing his cock deeper.

Then it happened. She was swept away to a place of bliss. Her body quivering in total abandon. Ecstasy rippling through her.

She moaned, the sound emanating from her raw and primal.

"Oh, baby, I love watching you come," Simon murmured against her temple.

She wrapped her arm around Simon's neck as Carter pulsed into her in lightning strokes, then drove deep and let out a guttural groan. She could feel him releasing into her body.

"Carter's coming inside me," she murmured to Simon.

"Fuck," Simon groaned.

Then she felt hot wetness on her hip as Simon also found his release.

Carter had slowed, but now rocked against her, driving her fading pleasure higher again. Bliss rocked through her to her core and she moaned again as another orgasm took her.

Finally, she fell back on the couch and sighed.

Simon leaned in and kissed her. She wrapped her arms around his neck and hugged him close.

"I seem to have made a mess on you. Let's go get you cleaned up."

Simon stood up and took her hand, then drew her to her feet. He led her to the bedroom, then into the en suite.

Carter turned the water on, then tugged her into the shower with him. As the warm water washed over her naked body, she watched Simon through the glass as he undressed. Carter scrubbed her body with his soapy hands, washing away Simon's seed. Simon stood on the other side of the glass door, naked except for the large bandage covering the burn on his torso and the wound on his thigh.

She frowned at the reminder of his injuries.

He reached for the door and she shook her head.

"No, you wait there," she said. "I don't want you to get your bandages wet."

He frowned, but she leaned against the glass, pressing her breasts tight. His eyes lit up at the view. Then Carter glided his hand around her and down her stomach to stroke her intimate flesh, his hardening cock pressing against her ass. She arched against his hand, feeling her arousal build.

As Simon watched, his cock hardened and rose.

"I think it's time to go to the bedroom." Her words came out deep and throaty.

Carter pulled her tight against his body, then pushed open the glass door. Simon greeted her with a towel and dried her off, thoroughly stroking every part of her with the thick, fluffy fabric. Then he tugged her into his arms and captured her mouth.

Simon's tongue drove deep, pulsing into her.

He took her hand and led her into the bedroom. She walked to the bed and leaned forward, offering herself to him, but he drew her up again and turned her toward him. He stroked her hair from her face and kissed her.

"No. I want you in my arms."

He guided her onto the bed until she was lying on her back. She opened her legs and he prowled over her.

"I want you inside me, Simon. I want you to make love to me."

"Yes," he said, his voice smooth as silk.

He pressed his hard cockhead against her slick flesh, his sapphire eyes glowing with need. He eased in slowly, his cock like molten steel, filling her in a smooth, easy stroke.

She squeezed around him, moaning at the feel of his hard shaft inside her.

"Oh, God, Simon. You feel so good."

He nuzzled her neck, his body resting on hers.

"So do you, sweetheart." He kissed her, his mouth moving tenderly on hers.

Carter stretched out on the bed beside her, laying on his side watching them.

Simon drew back, then glided deep again. This time he smiled and stroked back her hair, then took her hand and guided it to Carter's cock. He wrapped her fingers around it and she squeezed the thick column, to Carter's groan.

Simon drew back and glided deep again, making her insides quiver. She stroked up and down Carter's cock. She loved the feel of it pulsing in her hand as Simon's big cock filled her so deep.

Simon leaned in and nuzzled her neck again.

"Do you want both of us inside you, baby?" he asked.

The thought sent electricity surging through her.

"Oh, yes," she whispered.

Simon chuckled softly as he rolled to his side, his cock sliding from her body. Carter moved in close and rolled her toward him. Simon nuzzled the back of her neck, sending goose bumps dancing down her spine. Then he pressed his shaft against her ass. She arched back, feeling its length against her.

Simon pressed his cock between her thighs and pushed forward, stroking over her slick flesh. Then he glided back.

Carter's thick cockhead pressed against her wet slit and he slowly eased forward, stretching her even more than Simon had. Once Carter's hard shaft was all the way in, she felt Simon's slick cockhead press against her back opening. Slowly, Simon pushed forward, stretching her passage wide as he claimed her body in a sweet invasion. She squeezed around Carter, clinging to his shoulders as Simon moved deeper and deeper.

"Is he pushing inside your ass, baby?" Carter asked.

She nodded.

"Do you like that? Feeling his big cock inside you."

"Oh, yes," she moaned softly.

Simon was all the way inside now.

The two men held her between them, sandwiched in the warmth and protection of their big bodies. Oh, God, she loved being like this with them. Feeling totally possessed by them. And cherished.

She squeezed them inside her, their big cocks hard and ready to take her all the way to heaven.

Slowly, they began to move. Their solid members stroking inside her. Slowly. Moving deep into her. Then pulling back. Then gliding deep again.

"Ohhhhh, yessss," she moaned as the pleasure began to build. A slow delightful rise.

They kept filling her in a slow, even pace.

Then Carter surged deep into her, pressing her back

against Simon, making her gasp. Simon's long cock pushed impossibly deep inside her, making her quiver. Electricity danced along her nerve endings as she rode the rising wave.

She continued to cry out in pleasure, joy spiking through her as they thrust into her.

Delight blossomed and she moaned loud and long. Then her whole world burst into flames as an orgasm of epic proportions blasted through her.

As she clung to Carter's shoulders, moaning her release, he jerked forward and groaned. She felt the heat of him releasing inside her.

"Fuck, you feel good," Simon growled, then surged deep and erupted into her, too.

Her waning orgasm pulsed to a new peak at the feel of their hot seed filling her.

They kept rocking their hips, keeping her flying high, her moans going on and on, until she could hardly catch her breath. Then they took pity on her and slowed.

Simon chuckled, then brushed his lips along the back of her neck. She crumpled on the bed between them, basking in the glow of pleasure still washing through her.

As she sighed softly, Carter pulled her in closer and kissed her.

Simon rolled onto his back, followed by Carter. Rikki snuggled between them, the three of them a mass of tangled limbs.

She felt so warm and comfortable with them. So close. And she realized, no matter what her fears, no matter how difficult it might be to live with her worry about them getting hurt, she would find a way past it. Because living without them just wasn't an option.

She sighed again. "I love you. Both of you."

Carter pushed himself up on his elbow and gazed at her, his amber eyes glowing with warmth.

"I love you, too, sweetheart." His lips found hers and his tongue dipped deep, taking her breath away.

When he drew back, he stroked her hair from her face and smiled. Happiness blossomed deep inside her.

Then she gazed at Simon.

But he just lay quietly, his eyes closed.

Was he asleep? Did that mean he hadn't heard her?

She glanced at Carter uncertainly and he just shook his head and drew her close, holding her tenderly. She snuggled into him, trying to convince herself Simon was asleep. That he wasn't trying to avoid an awkward situation because he didn't feel the same way about her.

"What the hell was that last night?"

Simon glanced up from his coffee to face Carter's glare. Carter stood in the kitchen doorway glowering at him.

"Rikki says 'I love you' for the first time," Carter continued, his amber eyes sparking, "and you feign sleep."

Chapter Nineteen

Simon's chest constricted and he wanted to deny it, but he knew there was no point.

"Where's Rikki?" he asked.

"Don't worry. She's in the shower," Carter said, walking to the counter and pouring himself a cup of coffee. He sat down across from Simon. "This is exactly what we wanted. I thought you'd be as thrilled as I am."

Simon nodded. "Me, too. But now . . ." He shrugged. "I get it. I get why she's been so reluctant to get involved with someone she has to worry about losing. After getting just a taste of that when we thought she was in that burning building . . . the terror that we might have lost her . . ." His gaze locked with Carter's. "How can we ask her to suffer through that every single day?"

Carter shook his head. "We're not asking her to. She's in love with us. It comes with the territory."

"Unless we tell her we don't want something permanent. That this is just a fling and it's time to move on."

"Just like that? And won't she feel used and rejected?"

Simon hated the idea of lying to her, and his heart ached at the thought of hurting her.

"Not if we explain it right," Simon said, trying to convince himself as much as Carter. "Let her down easy."

Carter shook his head. "I don't want to explain it away. Or let her down at all. I'm in love with her and I want to go the distance. How the hell you can think of giving up what we have with her is beyond me."

Anger and frustration flared inside Simon. "Maybe I care about her well-being more than you do."

Carter jerked to his feet, his eyes blazing with fury.

But before he could utter a word, they both heard Rikki's footsteps in the hall. Carter's hands clenched into fists and he picked up his cup and headed to the patio doors, then disappeared onto the deck.

"Good morning," Rikki said when she stepped into the kitchen.

She looked all soft and feminine, despite wearing Carter's robe. Her freshly washed hair billowed over her shoulders in soft waves, shimmering in the sunlight.

"Good morning. Did you sleep well?" Simon asked as she poured herself a coffee.

She sat down and sipped the steaming brew, then nodded.

"You slept really well, too, I take it," she said as she set her cup down. "You must have been tired because you fell asleep right away last night."

He could see the anxiety in her eyes.

"Yeah, sorry about that. I guess between my injuries and the effect of the painkillers . . ." He shrugged.

He felt guilty about using the "I'm injured" card, but he wasn't ready to face the conversation head-on yet. And definitely not until he and Carter had come to some agreement.

Over the next few days, Rikki felt a distance growing between her and Simon. Carter was as affectionate and loving as ever—even more so since she'd confessed her love—but Simon seemed to be holding back. She also sensed friction between him and Carter.

She knew at some point she had to talk to them about Tony. With everything that had happened, they'd let the whole thing drop, but Tony was going to call her on his way home from his parents, intending to stop by and talk to her. But that was still a couple of weeks off, and now didn't seem a good time to bring it up.

Simon's leg and burns were healing nicely. The chief insisted he take the next shift off, but Simon was raring to go back to work on the following one.

Rikki accompanied the two of them to the station, ready to finish up the calendar. While she'd been staying with Carter and Simon, she'd spent a lot of time organizing the photos she'd taken and putting together a draft of the calendar for approval. She'd also chosen the best shots of Dodge from the ones she'd taken for the book covers and sent them to Cassie to present to her author client.

Rikki had arranged a meeting with the chief for ten o'clock and Cassie arrived an hour before that so they could go over the calendar together. Cassie loved what Rikki had done and when they showed it to the chief, along with Carter and Simon for approval, everyone was pleased with it. Rikki was thrilled they were happy with her work and relaxed while Cassie continued the meeting with talk of how they would promote the calendar.

After the meeting, Cassie stayed for lunch.

"Hey, I've got great news," Cassie said as they sat down at the table together.

Carter sat with them, but Simon was eating with Dodge and Tanner, catching up on what had been happening while he was gone.

"What's that?" Rikki asked.

"I have an erotica author who wants six of the photos you took of Dodge for her current book series."

Excitement surged through her. "That's great."

Cassie smiled. "And? Don't you want to know how much?"

Rikki nodded. She didn't care how much it was. She was just delighted that Cassie had been able to sell them.

"I told her that you would do an introductory price of eighteen hundred for the six, because she's your first client, and that includes a huge discount because they're all from the same shoot, but that in the future, it'll be more."

Rikki's jaw dropped. "That's a lot of money."

"Well, remember that you aren't paying the model this time. Dodge and the others are letting you do a free shoot with them because you volunteered to do the calendar. You insisted that in the future, you'll be paying them modeling fees."

Rikki had no idea how much she should pay for the modeling fee, but she'd learn about it and pay a fair amount.

"Cassie, I really appreciate it. I feel like I could make a career for myself in photography if I can keep this up."

Cassie was still grinning broadly. "And she's already booked you for six more covers for her next series. All from a single photo shoot again. Two thousand for the set."

Rikki sucked in a breath. "Oh, that's wonderful."

Cassie handed her an envelope she'd pulled from her purse.

"What's this?" Rikki asked.

"A check for the first set of photos and half up front for the second set."

Rikki opened the envelope and stared at the check. She turned to Carter with a big smile.

"I want to take you and Simon out to dinner tomorrow night to celebrate. And I want to pay you rent. Maybe we can talk to Simon about it right now so we can settle on an amount."

Carter and Simon had refused her offer of rent while she stayed with them, which had been a godsend because she didn't know when she'd get back the rent she'd already paid for the townhouse.

Carter frowned as he stared at his meal.

"I don't think we should do that today. I'm sure this first day back is wearing on him."

She glanced at the table where Simon was sitting with Dodge and Tanner, and they were laughing heartily.

"He seems to be fine," she pointed out.

Carter stared at her, his expression serious. "Just trust me. It's not the time."

He glanced at his watch, then stood up, his meal only half eaten.

"I have some paperwork I need to catch up on. I'll talk to you later."

Rikki watched as Carter walked away.

"Trouble in paradise?" Cassie asked.

Rikki sighed. "I told them I loved them and . . . well, Simon pretended to be asleep." She frowned. "Or maybe he was. I don't know. But I feel like he's been putting distance between us ever since."

"What did Carter say?"

Rikki smiled. "He said he loves me, too." Then her smile faded. "But you know it'll be a huge problem if I'm with just Carter. It would probably ruin their relationship and . . ." She dragged her finger along the tabletop, her heart pounding. "I want to be with both of them. I *love* both of them."

Cassie nodded, then placed her hand on Rikki's.

"It might not be what you think," Cassie said. "The guy was injured. Are you sure it's not just that he's recovering?"

"Maybe. I don't know." She lifted her gaze to Cassie's, her chest aching. "It's just that it took so much to get to the point where I could allow myself to love them. And I really thought they both felt the same about me." She bit her lip. "I don't want to lose them."

"Losing them has been your fear all along."

Rikki nodded. "I know. I just didn't expect it to be because Simon doesn't want me."

The next two days between their shifts, Simon spent most of the time out running errands and keeping busy. Rikki assumed that was on purpose to keep away from her.

To keep her mind off it, she decided to ask Carter if he'd pose for her for the new book covers. The author wanted another man with a tattoo, so Carter fit the bill perfectly. She thought the rose vine coiling down his arm would look amazingly sexy and romantic on a cover.

She started by snapping pictures of him shirtless in the backyard, taking advantage of the natural light. Then they moved into the house and he stripped down to his boxers. They quickly wound up in the bedroom and he teased her by easing his boxers down, but unlike Dodge's teasing during his photo shoot, Carter stripped them off entirely and tossed them aside.

She gazed hungrily at his swelling cock.

"You know I can't take pictures of you like that."

He chuckled. "Who says we need to keep taking pictures?"

She licked her lips, loving the idea of flinging off her own clothes and surging into his arms. Especially without the current tension of Simon making her feel cautious and uncomfortable.

She bit her lip. "As inviting as that is, I'd really love to get just a few more pictures."

"Okay." He pulled the bedspread off the bed and tossed it aside, then slipped under the sheets. "I'll make you a deal. I'll keep posing for you if you take the pictures naked."

"What?" Her cheeks flushed. "I can't do that."

"Why not? It's just the two of us here."

"I . . . uh . . ." Then she laughed. "Okay."

She put the camera down and stripped off her clothes, dropping them piece by piece onto the floor. When she grabbed her camera again and turned to him, the heat in his eyes was enough to curl her toes. A shiver ran down her spine.

"Actually," she said, her voice an octave lower, "this is perfect. You have that smoldering, sexy look in your eyes."

"Come over here and I'll show you just how smoldering hot things can get."

She laughed. "You promised me pictures first."

She snapped a couple as she moved slowly toward the bed. Man, these would sizzle right off the screen.

She walked to the side of the bed and rearranged the sheets in just the right way to hint at the growing erection he had under the covers and still be tasteful. She snapped a few more shots, intensely aware of his gaze on her naked breasts. Then she pulled the sheets a little lower. The sight of the trail of hair down his stomach, disappearing under the covers was intensely erotic.

Snap. Snap. Snap.

When she reached down to make another adjustment, he grabbed her wrist and pulled her onto the bed, his body beneath her. The feel of his hard, muscular planes sent her pulse rocketing. His lips found hers and his tongue swept inside. When she murmured her approval, he rolled her under him and held her arms above her head as he stared down at her, his amber eyes simmering.

"I love the feel of you beneath me."

She laughed softly. "And I love being here." She pushed her wrists against his hands, testing his strength. There's no way she'd break free of his hold unless he chose to let her go.

She arched upward, pressing her breasts against him. Her nipples were hard and aching. He dipped his head down and licked one, then sucked it into his mouth. The warmth . . . the soft suction . . . sent heat flooding through her.

"Ohhh, yes."

He suckled her other nipple and she moaned.

"I want you," she murmured.

He grasped both her wrists in one hand, then slid his other hand down her arm, over her breast, then lower.

When she felt his fingers glide over her intimate folds, she gasped. He pressed into her slickness, dipping his finger inside her.

"Fuck, you really do." He pressed his hot cockhead to her slick flesh and glided over it, teasing her. Then he centered it and pushed inside. Just a little.

"Oh, yes." She arched forward, inviting him in.

He pulsed forward in short, rhythmic strokes, barely pushing in past his cockhead.

"More. Please." She needed all of him.

He chuckled, then glided deep inside her, to her gasp of delight.

She clung to him, holding him close as they both revelled in the feel of him inside her.

Then he began to move. His cock sliding along her passage. In and out.

Her body ached, and she delighted in this carefree lovemaking. Just enjoying being with the man she loved.

At least, one of them.

Heat sizzled through her, electrical sparks crackling along her nerve endings.

"Yes."

He pulsed deep. A sudden wave of pleasure swelled inside her. Intense. Gripping.

"God. Faster. Please." She was nearly panting. She couldn't believe this was happening so fast.

He sped up, driving into her harder now.

"Oh . . . I'm . . . so . . . close." Her words came out in little gasps.

"Me, too, sweetheart." He ground his hips against her, then thrust faster. Deeper.

Her voice rose to a higher-pitched moan of delight as her whole body quivered. Nearing the edge.

Just as the first ripples of euphoria shimmered through her, the door opened. Simon stood in the doorway, his eyes dark and intense. Her gaze locked with his as the pleasure overtook her, then she gave herself over to it, the orgasm blossoming through her.

He watched her, his sapphire blue eyes turning dark as midnight.

"Ohhh, Carter. I'm . . . coming." The last word lingered

on a long, languid moan as she surrendered to the bliss. Floating on a wave of absolute joy.

"Oh, fuck, sweetheart. I love hearing you say that." His tone was gruff and he rode her, keeping her orgasm going on and on.

Then he groaned and his cock pulsed, filling her with heat.

Finally, they both collapsed on the bed. He kissed her tenderly, then rolled away, his gaze turning to Simon, who still watched, his stance rigid. As Simon's gaze glided down her body, she realized that wasn't the only thing that was rigid.

God, she wanted him, too. She opened her arms in invitation.

He hesitated only a second, then he surged toward the bed, shedding his clothes on the way. He swooped over her, now naked, and pulled her into his arms, his body tight against her as he kissed her. His tongue pulsed deep and he consumed her like a starving man.

She wrapped her hand around his swollen cock. It was hot and hard. And impossibly thick.

"I want you inside me." Her voice was hoarse and full of need.

He growled, then pressed his cock to her wet folds and thrust inside her. She gasped at his deep penetration.

"Oh, yes!" She nipped his earlobe. "Fuck me."

His blazing midnight eyes seared her senses. Her whole body began to quiver as he drew back. Then he thrust forward again. Filling her deep and hard.

She moaned, clinging to his broad shoulders.

"I'm going to make you come so hard, you'll never forget the feel of me inside you."

Then he thrust deep again. And before she could catch her breath, he thrust again.

He kept pounding into her, as if his life depended on it. Filling her over and over. The intimate stroking of his cock driving her wild with need.

"Oh yes, oh yes, oh yes," she kept chanting.

She trembled beneath his moving body, accepting every stroke of his cock with wild abandon. Loving the feel of him claiming her so completely.

"Are you close, baby?"

She nodded, unable to utter a word.

"Tell me," he demanded.

She tried and just croaked out a sound as pleasure vibrated through her.

"Tell me!" The command rippled through her, impossible to ignore.

"I'm going to come," she whispered against his ear, already feeling the first wave claiming her.

He thrust harder and she moaned.

"I'm . . . yes . . . Oh, God, I'm . . ." She moaned again. "Coming . . ."

Her voice seemed to vibrate with the pleasure and intensity of the release he was giving her. The orgasm swept over her and tumbled her into bliss. She felt lost in a euphoric swirl of delight.

She could feel her moans pulsing through her body and from her mouth, but the pleasure overrode her sense of time and space. There was only the feel of Simon's cock stroking her deeply. The pleasure rippling through her. And the swell of emotion at being possessed by him.

When he groaned his release, her body jolted into a new level of hyper pleasure and she lost her hold on reality altogether. Fading into darkness.

"Rikki! Are you all right?"

She opened her eyes to see Simon staring down at her. His cock was still embedded inside her and she squeezed around him.

"More than all right," she murmured, her voice husky. "I think I passed out. Is that even possible?"

His blue eyes, so filled with concern, darkened.

"Do you feel okay?" he grated. "I'm worried about you."

As he started to roll away, she curled her arms around him, but he still escaped.

"I'm fine, Simon. There's no need to worry. That was just so . . . intense."

She grabbed his biceps with both hands as he sat up.

"Please don't walk away," she said. "I want to know why you've been pulling away from me."

He frowned at her, then sighed. "All right."

"Simon, don't," Carter said in a sharp voice.

Simon locked gazes with Carter. "She deserves to know." He turned back to her. "Rikki, I think it's time we ended this between us."

Chapter Twenty

Rikki's heart lurched. "But why?"

"It's getting too serious and"—his gaze locked with hers and for a moment she saw a heartbreaking sadness—"I don't want you to get hurt."

"But I . . ." Tears swelled in her eyes and she blinked them back. She couldn't tell him she loved him now.

"For God's sake, Simon. Be honest with her."

She turned her gaze to Carter, then back to Simon.

"What's going on?"

"Fuck." Simon scowled. "Fine. I'm trying to protect you. After getting a taste of the intense worry of losing you, I realized why you decided not to fall for a firefighter again. You've already suffered so much pain that I can't put you in that position again."

"But it's not up to you to decide that for me."

"Except that we put you in this position. You told us you didn't want to get involved and we didn't listen. Therefore it *is* my responsibility."

She pushed herself onto her knees and rested her hand on his cheek, but he plucked it away and stood up.

"Please don't make this any harder than it already is," he said. "I want what's best for you. And I'm not it."

"You don't have to leave," Carter said as Rikki threw the few clothes she'd bought after the fire into a backpack.

"I can't stay here."

"I'll talk to him," Carter said. "We'll work this out."

She tossed the last thing in the bag, her heart pounding.

"Don't you see? I don't want anyone to have to talk Simon into wanting to be with me."

"But the man really does love you."

"Just not enough." She picked up the backpack and headed for the bedroom door.

Carter stepped in front of her. "What about you and me? You know I'm in love with you."

She paused, staring into his amber eyes, her heart compressing, then she raised her hand to his raspy cheek and stroked.

"And I love you. But how do we continue this without it totally destroying your relationship with Simon?"

"If he's going to be an idiot, then so be it, but I don't intend to give you up. And you love me." He tipped up her chin and captured her gaze. "The question is, do you love *me* enough?"

A riot of emotions swirled through her.

"Carter, right now I'm confused and hurt." She curled her fingers around his and squeezed. "Give me a few days to let this all sink in. I'm not saying good-bye. I just need a little time."

"I'll give you time. But not too much."

He took the backpack from her and put it on the floor, then pulled her into his arms. His kiss was passionate and heartrending. It was almost enough to make her dump her clothes back into the drawer and stay.

Almost.

Finally, he released her and picked up the backpack.

"At least let me drive you," he insisted.

"No, I've already called a cab."

She followed him down the stairs to the front door. Through the window, she could see the cab pulling into the driveway.

She took the bag from Carter's grip. Before she could turn away, he pulled her into a hug again.

"We'll talk soon," he said as he released her.

"Of course."

She grabbed her purse from the shelf by the front door and walked outside. When she got into the taxi, tears prickled at her eyes.

No matter what happened between her and Carter, she knew that losing Simon would leave a huge hole in her life.

Rikki knocked on Cassie's door. The moment Cassie opened the door and saw the tears shimmering in Rikki's eyes, she wrapped her arms around her and squeezed, then drew her inside.

"I didn't know where to go," Rikki said in a tremulous voice.

"You can always come here, honey. You know that."

Rikki just nodded as Cassie drew her into the living room. She dropped her purse and her hastily packed backpack onto the floor and they sat on the couch, Cassie's arm still around her.

"Now tell me what happened," Cassie said.

Rikki sucked in a shaky breath. "Simon ended it between us."

"Really?" She shook her head. "And what about Carter? What does he have to say about this?"

Rikki felt a tear trickle down her cheek. "He says he still wants to be with me . . ." She gazed at Cassie, her heart aching. "But if I stay with Carter, it'll tear the two of them apart. They've been friends a long time. I can't be the one responsible for destroying what they have."

"You know, you take a lot on yourself, honey. If you want to be with Carter and he wants to be with you, then it's not up to you to figure out what he needs, or what Simon needs, beyond that. They're big boys and can make their own decisions and figure out the consequences on their own."

Rikki stared down at her hands. "I don't know. Maybe you're right. I just can't think about it right now."

The pain of being rejected by Simon was too much. She loved him with all her heart and couldn't imagine going on without him.

Even if she had Carter.

"I don't have anywhere to go . . . now that the townhouse burned down . . ."

Cassie squeezed her tight.

"You're not going anywhere. You're staying right here. Like I told you when you moved here. I have a spare room and it's all yours."

Cassie had offered the room when Rikki had first moved here, but Rikki had wanted the adventure of finding a place and making it on her own, rather than just playing it safe and moving in with a friend. It had all been part of the excitement of making new friends and exploring a new town.

But now, she accepted it gladly.

"Thank you."

Cassie grabbed Rikki's backpack and led her up the stairs to the guest room.

"Make yourself at home. Right now, I think you could use some sleep."

Rikki nodded, feeling the exhaustion overwhelming her.

A knock on the door jarred Rikki from a deep sleep. She opened her eyes and gazed around blearily, a bit disoriented, then realized she was in the guest bedroom at Cassie's.

In her haze, she knew she had been in here for some time. Cassie had come in a couple of times insisting she eat something, and Rikki had nibbled a little, but then the pain reared up and she'd climbed under the covers and lost herself in sleep again.

A knock sounded again.

"Rikki," Cassie said from the other side of the door, "can I come in?"

"Yeah, of course." Rikki pushed herself up in the bed and rubbed her eyes.

The door opened and Cassie stepped inside, concern etched in her face.

"Honey, you've been holed up in here for days." Cassie walked to the window and opened the drapes.

Rikki blinked at the light streaming in the window, but it wasn't bright morning sunlight. It seemed to be the soft rays of early evening.

Cassie sat down beside her on the bed. She pushed Rikki's hair behind her ear.

"I know you need time to mourn, and that's okay. I'll give you whatever time you need. But right now, I want you to get in the shower and revive yourself, then come down and have something to eat. After that, if you feel like coming back up here again, that's okay." Cassie squeezed her hand. "Will you do that for me?"

"Yeah, sure." The last thing Rikki wanted to do was leave this room, but she wouldn't turn Cassie down. She knew Cassie was concerned about her.

Cassie smiled. "Good. See you downstairs in a few minutes."

After Cassie left, Rikki made her way to the shower, then fifteen minutes later, walked down the stairs dressed in her jeans, her hair damp but combed, carrying the plate from Cassie's latest attempt to feed her.

When she got to the kitchen, she put the plate in the dishwasher and glanced at the stove where Cassie had a pot of chili simmering.

"It'll be a few minutes yet," Cassie said. "So let's sit for a bit."

As soon as Rikki sat down on the couch, she could sense something was up.

"I just want to warn you," Cassie said, "that someone's coming over to see you in a few minutes. I told him it was okay."

Rikki's heart clenched. "Carter?"

He would try to talk her into continuing their relationship without Simon and she just wasn't ready to face that right now.

"No, it's not Carter."

Her stomach tied in a knot. Was it Simon?

But to go there would lead to too much pain. Because of course it wasn't Simon. He'd been very clear about not wanting her anymore.

The doorbell rang and her gaze jerked to the front door. A shadowy shape could be seen through the frosted glass of the door.

Whoever it was, he was tall and broad shouldered.

"Who is it?" she asked, butterflies fluttering through her stomach.

In answer, Cassie got up and went to the door. When she opened it, Rikki's breath caught.

It wasn't Simon. Or Carter.

Tony stood on the other side of the door.

Chapter Twenty-one

Rikki tried to calm her breathing as Tony introduced himself to Cassie and Cassie invited him in. Why was Tony here now? She thought he'd be in Florida with his parents for at least another week.

"Tony? What are you doing here?" she asked, glancing from Tony to Cassie.

"I invited him," Cassie said. "You left your purse down here and I know you've had several calls and texts in the past couple of days. But when it started ringing nonstop today, I decided I better answer it."

Cassie directed Tony to sit down. He chose the chair close to Rikki.

"Yeah, I've been texting you for a couple of days, telling you I was coming through town earlier than I'd planned. When I couldn't get through, I went to the townhouse you were living at last time I was here. Remember I dropped you off? But when I saw it had burned down . . . and you weren't answering . . . you can imagine how worried I was."

Her heart went out to him as she realized he must have thought she'd been hurt.

"I'm fine. I wasn't even in the house at the time."

He smiled. "I'm glad to hear that. And I'm happy you have a friend like Cassie to help you out."

Rikki realized that Cassie had disappeared, leaving the two of them alone in the room.

"So how was your visit with your parents?" Rikki asked.

He nodded. "It was good. They were happy to spend some time with me. Not happy about the circumstances, of course. They invited me to come live with them for a while, hoping I'll consider moving down there."

"And what did you say?"

He laughed. "Really? You think I want to be a grown man living with my folks? Even temporarily?"

"Sure. Why not? Your parents love you and they want to help you through a difficult time."

"You're right. I do appreciate that. But while I was down there, I got a call from the chief, and he said that he put in a good word for me and I've been offered a job as an arson investigator. That's why I'm going back early."

Rikki smiled. "That's great. I'm happy for you."

"Thank you." He leaned toward her and took her hand. "So this means I'll have regular hours and I won't be in danger on a daily basis like when I was a firefighter."

She glanced down at their joined hands, feeling a little uncomfortable, concerned about where this was going.

"So I was wondering," he went on, "if you might consider . . . maybe going out with me."

She drew her hand away. "Tony, we don't even live in

the same state, let alone the same city. That wouldn't really work."

He sent her a crooked smile. "Well, maybe you'd consider moving back to Ashton."

"Tony, I . . ."

"Or maybe we could keep it long distance at first to see if we think it'll work. It's not that long a drive from Ashton to Muldone. We could visit each other on weekends. And we could Skype regularly."

She glanced at him and she knew if she'd never met Simon and Carter, that she'd be interested in a relationship with Tony. He was a great guy and there was definitely an attraction between them.

But she knew what real love felt like. First with Jesse, and now with Simon and Carter. Whatever she could find with Tony wouldn't be enough.

"I'm sorry, Tony. You're a really great guy, and—"

He threw up his hands. "Okay, whoa. I don't need the 'Hey, you're a great guy' speech. And after that, you'll go on to say we can be friends."

She took his hand again. "Well, we are friends. I hope that won't change."

He sighed and nodded, then squeezed her hand.

"So no chance at all?" he asked.

She compressed her lips and shook her head.

"So you're seeing someone here I take it?" Tony asked. "Is he treating you right?"

She bit her lip. "It's complicated. You'll probably be shocked, but . . ." She sucked in a deep breath. "I'm actually seeing two guys. Close friends."

His eyebrows rose. "Really? That does sound complicated."

She bit her lip and as hard as she tried, she couldn't stop the tears from welling up.

"Okay. What's going on?" Tony asked.

She tightened her hand in his, needing the comfort, even though she didn't deserve it from this great guy she'd just rejected.

She told him about her struggle to get past her fear of being with a firefighter. And how she thought she'd made strides forward. But how Simon had been affected by the fear of believing she was in the townhouse when it burned down, and had thought she'd been hurt. Then how he'd turned her away afterward . . . for her own good.

"I hate to say this," Tony said, "but he sounds like a decent guy."

She nodded. "He is."

"What about the other man?"

"He wanted to stay with me, even without Simon, but that would destroy their friendship and I don't want to be the cause of that."

"You really love them, don't you?"

"I do, but I've lost them." Tears streamed down her face now.

Tony moved to the couch beside her and took her in his arms. She leaned against his hard chest, settling into his comforting embrace.

"I don't know about that," Tony said. "Let me ask you something."

As Simon pulled into the driveway his jaw clenched, his gaze locked on the car sitting in front of them.

"What the fuck!"

"Don't get bent out of shape," Carter said.

"It has a goddamned Ohio licence plate!" He jerked the car door open and strode to the front door, then knocked, his heart thudding in his chest.

"Just stay calm," Carter said in a soothing voice.

But how could he stay calm? No sooner had Rikki left his arms than she was with this other guy from her past. The one who could offer her love without the pain of believing she might lose him every single day when he went into work.

Moments passed, and he knocked again, louder this time. He saw movement behind the frosted glass, then the door opened.

"Simon?" Cassie said. "And Carter. I'm surprised to see you here."

Her voice had an edge of ice.

"We're here to see Rikki," Simon said.

"Yes, well, I'm not sure Rikki is ready to see *you*," she said, crossing her arms.

But Simon peered behind her and caught a glimpse of Rikki in the living room. In a deep embrace with another man.

"What the hell is going on?" he demanded, his voice level rising.

Rikki pulled from the man's arms and turned in his direction.

"Simon?" She stood up and walked toward the door. "It's okay, Cassie. Let them in."

Cassie stepped back and he surged into the house, Carter close behind him.

As he moved closer, he saw that Rikki's eyes were shimmering. She pushed back her hair, but he could tell the gesture was to camouflage her wiping away an errant tear.

Fuck! What the hell would he say now?

"What are you doing here, Simon?" she asked.

He glared at the other man, his teeth gritted.

"The question is, what are you doing here with him?"

She frowned. "What concern is it to you? You broke up with me. Remember?"

He sucked in a deep breath, then let it out.

"Yeah, and I was an idiot. You're a damn sight smarter than me, so I thought you'd have figured that out."

He stepped forward, wanting desperately to touch her. How could he ever have thought he could give her up?

"What are you trying to tell me, Simon?" she asked softly.

"I'm trying to tell you that I don't want to let you go. My life is empty without you. I need you in my life."

She tipped her head. "But you said that you couldn't let me live in fear like that. That you were doing it for my own good."

"That's true. And I'm a selfish prick because I can't let you go. I'll do anything to convince you to come back to me and Carter."

She stared at him and his gut clenched. He couldn't read

her expression. His heart pounded, ticking off the seconds, waiting for her to say something.

Anything.

"Well," she said, her voice a mere breath. "I'm selfish, too."

At that instant, his whole world came crashing down.

She was going to walk away.

Chapter Twenty-two

Rikki gestured to the man behind her. "This is Tony, from my hometown. I told you about him."

Simon gave the man a curt nod. Tony stood up and pushed his hands in his pockets, but didn't move closer.

The guy was good-looking, as well as having the muscular build that appealed to most women. Simon was sure he'd fucking lost Rikki.

"Tony and I have been talking and he asked me an important question."

"And what's that?" Simon asked through gritted teeth. Though he was sure he knew.

"He asked me if I had it to do again, would I give up my time with Jesse, knowing I was going to lose him. Knowing the pain I'd have to endure."

Her words stripped him of the arguments he'd been pulling together in his head to convince her she shouldn't marry this guy.

She took a step closer, her eyes filled with an emotion he couldn't read.

"And what did you tell him?" Simon asked softly, his chest compressing.

She shook head. Then her delicate fingers wrapped around his, making him quake with need.

"I told him that I wouldn't. Because every moment with Jesse was precious. I wouldn't give up a single one."

She squeezed Simon's hand and her eyes glowed.

"And I don't want to give up a single precious moment with you, either. Life is fleeting and we should live every moment for today. If I have you for only a few days, or years . . ." She stepped closer and stroked his cheek, gazing deeply into his eyes. "Or a lifetime, I don't want to give up a single precious moment of what we could share together."

His heart burst in joy and he pulled her into his arms.

"Oh, God, Rikki. I love you so much."

She tipped her head up, her eyes glistening. "And I love you."

Rikki's heart swelled with happiness as Simon's mouth found hers. His hand cupped her face and his kiss . . . tender and passionate . . . took her breath away. Tears flowed down her face, but this time, they were tears of joy.

She melted against him, opening to his gently prodding tongue and welcomed him inside. He stroked and teased until she was breathless with need.

When he finally drew back, the fire in his eyes set her insides ablaze.

"Hey, I'm feeling a little left out here," Carter said.

She laughed then moved into his arms. He kissed her with just as much passion and she could hardly believe that she had two wonderful men like this in love with her and wanting her in their lives.

Finally, their lips parted and she gazed up at Carter's beaming face with a smile, then stroked his cheek tenderly, telling him with her eyes that she appreciated that he'd been willing to stay by her side no matter what.

Then she drew back and turned to Tony. He stepped toward her.

"Tony, thank you." She stepped forward and gave him a big hug. His arms were tentative around her, but she squeezed and he tightened them. She could sense a little jealousy from Simon, but he didn't say anything.

"I'm sorry it didn't work out between you and me, but I really appreciate what you've done for me."

He smiled his crooked smile. "I want you to be happy," he said simply.

But the pain in his eyes broke her heart.

"I know how much pain you suffered after losing Jesse," Tony said, "and I'm glad I was able to help you take an important step to find happiness again."

He glanced at Simon and Carter.

"Take good care of her, or I'll be back here to kick both your sorry butts."

Carter grinned. "You and who else?"

Tony laughed. "Me and my entire crew."

Carter offered his hand and they shook.

"Really, man, we appreciate what you've done."

Then Simon stepped forward and shook Tony's hand silently. But they exchanged a nod that said far more than words ever could.

"Okay, I'll be on my way," Tony said.

"Oh, but why don't you join us for dinner or a drink before you go?" Rikki asked.

He grinned sheepishly. "I'd love to, bunny, but I think the three of you have some catching up to do."

Tony turned to the door, but not before Rikki saw the sadness in his eyes.

"Good-bye, Tony," she said.

Without turning around, Tony opened the door. "Good-bye, Rikki."

Then the door closed behind him.

As her heart ached for him, Carter's eyebrow shot up. "Bunny?"

She turned to him, then laughed. "Yeah, I'll tell you about it sometime."

Cassie came down the stairs with Rikki's backpack in her hand, then held it out to Carter.

"It's all packed. Now you two take her home and make up properly. Okay?"

Carter laughed, taking the backpack and walking to the door, then picking up Rikki's purse.

"Sounds like a great plan to me," Carter said.

Simon's brooding eyes turned to Cassie. "Thanks for looking out for her, Cassie."

"Of course," she said with a smile.

Then Simon took Rikki's hand and led her out the front door.

*   *   *

Rikki followed Simon and Carter into their house, Simon's hand snugly around hers. As soon as they got in the door, Simon dropped her backpack on the floor.

"Come here," he said in a low growl.

He grabbed her hand and pulled her against him. His lips found hers and she melted into his welcome embrace.

"I heard something about making up?" Carter said from behind her as he gathered her long hair in his hand and stroked it.

Simon's lips parted from hers and his gaze never left hers as he spoke.

"Yeah. I'm the one who has to make up to her. You, as I recall, didn't do anything wrong."

Carter laughed. "If you think that means I don't get in on the makeup sex, you're crazy."

"Well, Simon is right. He does have a lot to make up for," Rikki said in a teasing tone.

But Simon's eyes grew intense and her breath caught.

"Baby, I'm so sorry for pushing you away."

Her chest tightened and she brushed her lips against the rough stubble on his chin.

"I know you only did it because you care about me." She cupped his cheeks, gazing deep into the midnight depths of his eyes. "I'm just glad you finally realized—just like I did—that what's best for me is being with the two men I love."

He clutched her tighter to him, knocking the breath from her lungs.

"Fuck, baby, I love you so much. I'm just glad you'll

have me after that idiot move of mine." He tipped up her chin, locking gazes with her. "I never want to let you go."

She stroked his raspy jaw. "I love you so much."

He took her hand and dragged her across the room to the couch. He sat down, pulling her in close beside him. Carter sat on her other side.

Simon stripped her T-shirt over her head, then unfastened her bra.

Carter stroked his hands along Rikki's shoulders and nuzzled her neck as Simon eased the bra away. Carter's gaze locked on the fabric as it slid lower, exposing her chest, then the swell of her breasts.

Simon's fingertips glided over the soft flesh, sending tingles through her. Then he pressed her back against the couch and leaned in to take one hard nipple into his mouth. The feel of his heat around her, his tongue lapping over her sensitive bud, took her breath away.

She glided her hand over Simon's dark, bristly hair. Carter's heated gaze was locked on her exposed breast, slipping occasionally to Simon's lips wrapped around the other one.

"It feels so good having Simon suck my breast," she said as she reached for Carter's hand.

She placed it flat on her other breast, entwining her fingers with his as she pressed him against the soft flesh. Simon stood up and stripped off his clothes, dropping them to the ground. He was totally naked now, his cock pointing straight toward her.

"Oh, look at how big Simon's cock is." She wrapped one hand around the thick column. It pulsed in her grip.

"Mmm, I wish I had my hand around your cock, too," she said, keeping Carter's hand pressed firmly against her breast.

As she stroked Simon's rigid member, she leaned her head closer to Carter and kissed his shoulder. He turned his body and leaned in to kiss her, his tongue darting into her mouth.

She murmured softly into the kiss. Then she drew away and bent forward to press Simon's cockhead against her lips. She kissed it, then pushed out her tongue and made a show of licking the mushroom-shaped tip. Over the top and around the sides, even curling her tongue underneath.

"Carter, imagine I'm doing this to you."

"Oh, I am, baby." His words were a deep, throaty rumble.

She licked and licked, then opened her lips around the column of flesh and drew it slowly inside. The big cock-head filled her mouth. She sucked on it, her cheeks hollow-ing. She heard a catch in Carter's breathing.

Equal parts heat and joy filled her at the thought she was giving both her men pleasure.

She glided downward on Simon's cock, taking him deeper and deeper. When she'd taken him as far as she could, she drew back again. Then she plunged downward again.

Simon's breathing was speeding up and his fingers glided through her hair, drawing it away from her face so Carter could see her. Could see the big column of flesh filling her mouth again and again.

"Fuck, you two are torturing me," Carter groaned. "Who knew being the good guy meant having to suffer the most?"

She eased off Simon's cock, stroking it with her hand and grinning at him.

"Do you want us to stop?"

Carter shook his head. "God, no."

She laughed and stroked his cheek. "You're right. You have been pretty sweet to me. Maybe it's not fair that I give Simon all the attention."

She released Simon's cock and stood in front of Carter. Then she unzipped her jeans and pushed them to the floor, along with her panties.

Carter's hot gaze traveled the length of her naked body, his breathing labored. She leaned forward and he covered her breast, squeezing gently. His fingertips teased her hard nipple and she murmured in approval. Then his mouth found it and she moaned softly.

His tongue teased her sensitive bud, swirling over it . . . flicking . . . then swirling again. Wild sensations fluttered through her body; then when he suckled, they burst through her, straight to her core. She could feel wetness pooling between her legs and wanted to climb onto his lap right then and take him deep inside her, then ride him to heaven.

Instead, she wrapped her hand around his head, her fingers twining in his soft waves of hair and held him tight to her.

When he released her, his hand trailing over her damp breast, she stood up and stroked her hand over his chest, then dug her fingertips into the fabric of his T-shirt and gripped it in her fist.

"I think it's time for you to take these clothes off," she said, tugging the shirt upward.

He whipped it over his head, then unfastened his jeans and flung them off.

She laughed at his enthusiasm. As he sank back onto the couch, she gazed at his big, thick cock standing straight up.

She knelt in front of him and wrapped her hand around it with a sigh.

Simon moved behind her and his hands glided around her body. He cupped her breasts, until her nipples were so hard they felt like they'd burst. Then he opened his fingers enough so they peeked out.

"Fuck, that is so sexy," Carter murmured.

His cock swelled in her hand and she stroked up and down.

"I've missed being with you like this." Her voice sounded like hot silk. "I want to taste you so badly."

She leaned forward and pressed her lips to Carter's hot, hard cockhead. As she took him inside, moving deeper and deeper on his long column, he groaned.

"Oh, fuck, baby, that feels so good." His voice dropped to a low murmur. "And what would make it even better is if I could watch Simon fuck you."

She drew back and glanced over her shoulder to see Simon stroke his erection, his hand gliding its length.

"I think that can be arranged," Simon said. "But first we need to warm her up."

"She seems pretty fucking hot to me right now," Carter countered.

Simon laughed then pressed the side of his shaft against her ass and pivoted his hips. Both she and Carter could see the long cock gliding up and down, the head rising up over her ass, then disappearing again. At the feel of it stroking her ass, she longed to feel it inside her.

Then he switched angles and his cock caressed her slick petals. She moaned at the exquisite sensation.

"Is he inside you?" Carter demanded.

Simon chuckled and pulled Rikki to her feet, then turned her to face him. He bent her down in front of him, her legs still straight and her ass in the air, her intimate flesh totally exposed to Carter, and pressed his cockhead to her lips. She opened and took him inside.

Then she felt something soft and warm touching her intimate flesh. Carter was licking her. She hiked her ass higher and opened her legs more, giving him better access. He chuckled and then his mouth covered her. She pumped up and down on Simon's cock as Carter pressed his tongue deep inside her. Soon, he'd found her clit and was teasing it mercilessly.

She began to quiver, pleasure humming through her. Simon eased her off his cock and pressed her head to his stomach, holding her steady as Carter glided his fingers over her slick flesh. He suckled her clit as he pressed two fingers inside her. Soon he was thrusting and she felt pleasure spike through her.

She gasped at the rising joy within her.

She moaned at the delightful shimmer of sensations.

"Ohhh, Carter. I'm so close."

"That's right baby," Simon said, stroking her hair. "I want to see you coming because Carter is sucking your clit and finger fucking you."

The swell of sensations swept her away, her body pulsing in a primal surge of euphoria.

She let out a long, mournful wail of pleasure.

When her orgasm waned, she leaned against Simon, barely keeping on her feet.

"Fuck, I'm so close it wouldn't take much," Carter said, his hand firmly around his cock, stroking it.

"Then why don't we try this?" Simon asked and eased Rikki backward.

She clung to Simon's arms as he lowered her onto Carter's lap. The feel of Carter's cock brushing against her folds made her moan.

Simon lowered her more and she sucked in a breath at the feel of Carter's thick cock filling her. When it was all the way inside and she was sitting on his lap, she couldn't help but squeeze him inside her, to his groan.

She laughed, squeezing again to his moan. He said it wouldn't take much, so she decided to tease him by giving him only the smallest of movements.

Simon pressed his cock to her lips and she opened for him. He glided deep into her mouth. Carter's hand covered her breast and caressed.

"Baby," Carter murmured, "I'm so close."

She squeezed again, rocking a little this time. She loved teasing him like this.

"Oh fuck yeah."

She squeezed faster and rocked. Carter watched Simon's cock glide in and out of her mouth, his eyes glazing.

"Fuck. I'm. So. Close."

She squeezed and arched her back, at the same time cupping Simon's balls while taking his cock deep.

Carter groaned and she felt him erupt inside her. At the sensation of his hot seed filling her, she felt an orgasm explode inside her, too. Simon pulled free of her mouth, his big hand stroking his own cock as he watched her.

She moaned her pleasure. Carter's finger found her clit and he stroked it, driving her higher and higher until she blasted into ecstatic heights.

Finally, she gasped, then exhaled and fell forward, resting against Simon's stomach.

Carter's lips trailed along her back.

"I still want to watch Simon fuck you," Carter murmured against her skin.

"No problem." Simon pulled the large ottoman in front of Carter.

Simon drew her to her feet, then she felt herself floating downward as he lowered her to the ottoman. He knelt in front of her and wrapped his hand around his thick cock. It was pulsing with need.

"You want to watch my cock drive into her?" he asked Carter.

"Fuck, yeah."

His hot cockhead brushed her sensitive petals and she longed for it inside her. The swollen head pushed inside, sending vibrations of pleasure rocketing through her.

"Oh, yes. Fuck me, Simon," she begged.

He drove forward, filling her with one thrust. She moaned at the incredible sensation.

He drew back and thrust forward again.

She wrapped her hand around his shoulders and he leaned in, then kissed her tenderly.

"I love you, sweetheart," Simon said. "We both do."

"I know," she murmured softly. "And I love you both. I always will."

He laughed in joy, then began thrusting. Driving his hard cock into her again and again. A deep well of pleasure pulsed within her, expanding with each thrust. Thrumming through her body. She quivered in his arms, moaning against his ear.

"Fuck, I love those soft sounds you make," Simon said, then kissed her temple.

Then he thrust deep and hard. He filled her like a jackhammer, shaking her loose from reality and flinging her over the edge. She moaned as she exploded in sheer ecstasy. Her wails filled the room and she shot to a new level of euphoria.

Still he kept pumping into her. Then he drove deep and groaned his release. She tightened around him, her whole world imploding, then exploding again into blissful abandon.

Finally, she collapsed on the ottoman, gasping for air.

"Fuck, I'll never get tired of watching you two," Carter said.

She smiled at him as Simon rolled away. "Watching is fun."

She stroked her hands over her breasts, then squeezed her hard nipples. Carter's cock twitched and slowly inflated like a balloon.

"But I think it's time for a little more participation."

She glided her fingers over her wet folds, amazed at how easy it was to coax an erection from her sexy lovers. Licking her lips as she stared at his thick column, she held out her hand to him.

Carter surged forward from the couch to his knees, his amber eyes filled with hunger. He grabbed her hand and sucked her wet fingers into his mouth. As he drew on them deeply, she arched her hips.

"I want you inside me," she murmured, her voice filled with need. "I want you to fuck me."

The rumbling chuckle from deep in his chest drove her need even higher. He pressed his hard cockhead to her opening, then glided into her. She squeezed, welcoming him, as he filled her all the way.

She clung to him, holding his body tight to hers.

"Is that what you wanted, baby?" Carter whispered against her ear.

She nodded, so close to the edge already she could barely think straight.

Then he started to move. He drew back in a slow, steady stroke, then glided deep again.

"Ohhh, yes." Her raspy words were hoarse against his ear.

He picked up speed, his cock filling her again and again. She rose to meet him, grinding her hips against his with each thrust, the pleasure quivering through her whole body.

"Ah, fuck, baby. I'm going to come again."

Carter kept pounding into her and she moaned at the delightful shimmer of sensations.

Then she blasted into sheer joy, an orgasm claiming her in sudden and euphoric ecstasy.

They both collapsed on the ottoman, panting. After a few minutes, Carter kissed her soundly, then drew her to her feet. He took her hand and led her into the bedroom, Simon on their heels.

A moment later, she was snuggled in bed between these two wonderful men, each of them with an arm around her waist. Simon's lips trailed along her neck while Carter nuzzled her ear.

She was sure she wouldn't be getting much sleep tonight.

"I'm so glad we've worked this out. I can't imagine my life without you," Simon said.

Carter pulled her tighter. "Me, too."

She sighed. "Well, no worries there, because this is exactly where I want to be. Always."

WITHDRAWN

Oswego Country Public Library
120 Nickerson St.
Oswego, IL 60543
www.oswego.lib.il.us